KING ARTHUR
AND THE
KNIGHTS OF THE ROUND TABLE

KING ARTHUR
AND THE
KNIGHTS OF THE ROUND TABLE

Linda Yeatman

Illustrated by Llewellyn Thomas

Heinemann · London

For Catherine, Lucy and Rosanna

First published 1991 by
William Heinemann Ltd
Michelin House
81 Fulham Road, London SW3 6RB
London · Melbourne · Auckland

An Albion Book

ISBN 0 434 97702 0

Typesetting and colour origination by York House, London
Printed and bound by Printer Industria Grafica S.A., Barcelona, Spain

CONTENTS

1

THE SWORD IN THE CHURCHYARD

Since the death of Uther Pendragon there had been no high king. Dark days had fallen across the land. King fought king, lord fought lord, and many went hungry and cold. Enemies from across the seas raided and stole, and there was safety for no man.

It was said that a dragon's head had been seen in the sky, swirling and mingling with the stars, and this was a sign that Uther's son would rule the land as a great high king, more powerful than even his father before him. But who knew where Uther's son might be, if indeed he lived at all. Whispers travelled from town to town and castle to castle that he had been spirited away at birth by the magician Merlin, but none knew when he would be revealed, or how they would recognise him as Pendragon's son when he came.

Some decided they could wait no longer for the dragon prophecy to be fulfilled, and so on Christmas Day a meeting was called of all the mighty men in England. They came to London so they might choose a new high king. The Archbishop held a service in the great church and while they prayed a strange and mysterious thing happened.

A huge block of stone appeared in the churchyard. On top was a metal anvil, and set right through the metal, point down, gleamed a great shining sword. Around the stone, in gold letters was written:

WHOSO PULLS THIS SWORD FROM THE STONE AND
ANVIL IS THE RIGHTFUL KING OF ALL ENGLAND.

"A sign, a sign at last," they said. "Now we will find our new high king."

But the Archbishop declared, "Let no man pull out the sword until the service is over."

He need not have spoken, for after the service it was found that no one present, not one of the kings or nobles, could move the sword. It was stuck fast. Many tried, heaving and tugging, but it stayed gripped firmly in place. So a great tournament was planned for the following week, in the hopes that one of those who came might pull out the sword and prove himself the future high king of England.

* * *

It was early on New Year's Day when knights and their squires made their way to the jousting ground. Nobles and knights had come from all over England to test their mettle. The wintry sun shone clear and bright and the frost on the ground matched the crackle of excitement in the air. Many young men were riding for the first time to such a great tournament, and among them was a new made knight, Sir Kay, and his young brother Arthur.

"Look, Arthur," called Sir Kay, "you can see the tents and pavilions through the trees. We're nearly there. I hope we're not going to be late for the first joust."

They followed their father, Sir Ector, past the churchyard towards the jousting ground. They scarcely glanced at the mysterious sword for they were in such a hurry. Young Arthur had not even heard the story about it. Like many of the other squires he was too excited about attending such a magnificent tournament to pay much attention to stories circulating amongst the lords and knights.

At the jousting ground Sir Kay found he was due to fight in one of the early rounds. "My sword!" he cried suddenly, "I have not got it with me. I must have left it behind. How could I be so careless!"

"I'll go and fetch it," Arthur said at once, and jumping on his horse, he hurried back the way they had come. Too late! The house where they were staying was locked. Arthur banged and rattled on the door, but everyone, including all the women and servants, had gone to watch the jousting.

"Poor Kay, he'll miss his fight if I cannot get him a sword," thought

Arthur, as he rode back with the bad news. As he passed the church-yard, he noticed the sword standing there, its hilt gleaming in the winter sunlight, and thought, "Why don't I take that one? No one else is using it."

He entered the churchyard and placing his hand on the sword's hilt, he pulled. As a hot blade might slip through snow, the sword slid smoothly from the metal.

Arthur was in too much of a hurry to read the words written around the stone. He took the sword quickly to Sir Kay who was waiting impatiently at the tournament ground.

Sir Kay saw at a glance that it was not his own sword. Then he realised that it was the sword from the churchyard, for like many of the knights he had attempted the day before to pull it from the grip of iron that held it.

With a swift decision, he strode over to Sir Ector and said, "Look, Father, here is the sword from the churchyard. I must be the rightful king of all England!"

"How did you get this sword, my son?" asked an amazed Sir Ector.

"I pulled it out from the anvil on the stone in the churchyard."

Suspecting that his son was not telling the truth, Sir Ector called Arthur, and he took both young men to the church, where he asked Sir Kay to swear how he had got the sword.

Sir Kay knew now he could not hide the truth from his father, and said, "It was brought to me by my brother Arthur, who had gone to fetch my own sword, which I carelessly left behind."

Sir Ector said to Arthur, "Show us what you did."

Arthur, puzzled and anxious that he might have done wrong, re-placed the sword in the anvil and the stone. Before he could pull it out again Sir Ector and Sir Kay both tried. Neither could move the sword. Then Arthur took the hilt as he had before, and again the sword answered to his touch. He stood before them, holding it in his hands.

Now Sir Ector knelt before Arthur, and bowing his head, said, "I know now that you, and only you, Arthur, are the true-born king of this land."

"What are you saying, Father?" Arthur asked, "and why do you kneel before me? How can I be the rightful king when you and my brother Kay are still alive? In any case we are not great or important people like many at the tournament today."

"I have never told you before, Arthur, but the truth is you are not my son. Many years ago, when you were still a tiny baby, Merlin, the magician, brought you to us. He asked us to bring you up as though you were our own son, with Kay here as your brother. I have never known who your real parents were."

"I shall always think of you as my father, whoever I am. If I am to be king, what can I do to thank you?" Arthur asked.

"I look for no thanks, Arthur, except that when you rule this land remember your foster brother Kay, and reward him by making him your High Steward. He will serve you with loyalty. But come, we must tell the Archbishop and the great lords at the tournament that you are the rightful king, for you are the one to pull out the sword in the churchyard."

The nobles were angry and jealous when they heard that a boy, not yet old enough to grow a beard, was to be proclaimed their king, and they refused to accept Arthur. On Twelfth Night they all attempted again, in turn, to pull the sword from its resting place, sure that if a boy could do it, so could they. But none except Arthur could move the sword – and for him it was easy.

Still they would not accept him but decided to wait a few weeks and hold yet another competition at Candlemass. Meanwhile a great tent was erected in the churchyard around the sword which was left thrust through the anvil into the great slab of stone. Ten men were set to guard it, five by day and five by night.

Once more, at Candlemass, no one but Arthur could pull the sword from the anvil. Once more the mighty men disagreed amongst themselves and refused to accept Arthur as their king. "We will have another contest at Easter," they decided.

Now Merlin advised Sir Ector, "Place loyal and brave men around Arthur to protect him. Some who do not want him as their king might plot to kill him before Easter." And so men loyal to Arthur stayed near him and guarded him. These included Sir Kay, his foster brother, Sir Bedivere, and some of the knights who had been faithful followers of the old king, Uther Pendragon.

Again at Easter no lord or knight could pull out the sword except, of course, Arthur, and once more the decision to accept him as their king was delayed, this time until Whitsun.

At Whitsun a large crowd gathered in London. Now, when Arthur pulled the sword from the anvil and the stone in the churchyard, the mass of people called out, "We will have Arthur! Arthur for king!" The Archbishop saw that no amount of delay would change the situation, so while many of the nobles still grumbled, Arthur knelt before the Archbishop. He swore to serve God and the people of the land. He was knighted and now many of the great lords and knights knelt before him and swore loyalty to him.

"King Arthur! King Arthur! Welcome King Arthur!" the crowd shouted.

This is how Arthur became king. At first he was only king in name. It was the task of this mere boy to bring peace to a warring land, to quell his enemies and to make Britain strong again. In doing so, he forged a legend that will never die, the legend of King Arthur and the Knights of the Round Table.

2

ARTHUR'S CHILDHOOD

"Tell me, Merlin," Arthur demanded, "tell me why I am king and how the sword came into the stone. I want to know about my family and why I was brought up as Sir Ector's son. Why? Why?"

"It's a strange tale, and I'll tell you, but all in good time," Merlin replied.

"You're always full of mysteries and secrets, Merlin. Perhaps you should start by telling me who you are and why you know so much."

Merlin, the priest of ancient magic, the wise man, who could see events in the future, looked at the eager youth before him, and saw the time had come to talk. So, with Arthur's great white hound, Cabal, stretched out between them on the hearth, the old man and the young king settled either side of the fire.

"Sixteen years ago," Merlin began, "your father, Uther Pendragon, high king of England, called his followers to a council in London. Among them came Gorlois, Duke of Cornwall, who brought with him his beautiful wife Igraine. As soon as he saw her, the king loved Igraine. She could see how he felt, and realising it could be dangerous to be loved by the king, she went to her husband. 'Take me away from here before any harm is done. The king loves me and wants me to be with him all the time.'

" 'We'll return to Cornwall at once,' said Gorlois, and he and his household left London and rode back to the west country.

"King Uther was enraged, and called his fighting men around him. 'We must go after Duke Gorlois of Cornwall. He has insulted me by returning home before we had finished our council.'

"In Cornwall, Duke Gorlois heard the king was following with his

16

army, so he placed Igraine in the castle of Tintagel. The name means 'almost an island', and if you ever go there, Arthur, you will see what a strong fortress it is, for it is built out into the sea, with only a narrow causeway from the land for its entrance. Gorlois planned that Igraine should stay in Tintagel, safe from the king and any fighting, while he prepared to defend himself from another castle nearby.

"It was, you must understand, a very sad situation, for King Uther, a great king and a fine warrior, loved Igraine to distraction. He had no wife and he needed an heir, yet the woman he loved was the wife of one of his allies. He called me to him one day, and told me of this love for Igraine which was driving him crazy. 'Use your magic arts, Merlin,' he begged. 'I need them now as never before.'

"I knew, for I have always had the gift of seeing into the future, that a son would be born to Uther and Igraine, a son who would be a mighty king, the wisest and strongest ever to rule this kingdom. And so I agreed to help. I have long been skilful at disguise, it is a most useful art, and that night I surpassed myself. I made myself look like Gorlois' most trusted servant, while Uther became indistinguishable from Gorlois himself. Together we rode under cover of dark to Tintagel. At the gate we called out to the guards, imitating Gorlois' voice announcing that the duke wanted to visit his lady.

"We were admitted, and I waited while the king spent some hours in Igraine's rooms. I knew that Gorlois himself had planned to attack the king's castle that same evening, so there was no danger of his coming to Tintagel too. But what we did not know was that in this attack Duke Gorlois himself was slain. As we rode out from Tintagel in that dark hour before dawn, a messenger passed us, bent low over his horse's neck, riding with speed towards Tintagel. We hid in some trees as he thundered past.

"'What could bring the duke's messenger so fast?' the king whispered.

"I had a strange foreboding. He rode, as you can guess, to tell Igraine that her husband, Gorlois, had died that night.

"When Igraine was told, she asked, 'How can this be, for my lord spent the night with me?'"

"What a wicked trick of fate that was for King Uther. Whether or not we had used my skills of disguise for him to visit Igraine, her husband would have died that night."

Merlin paused in his story, and Arthur stared into the fire. "I still don't understand," he said at last. "Are you telling me I am the child of Uther and Igraine? If so, why was I brought up as Sir Ector's son?"

"Listen," said Merlin, "and I'll tell you of another night at Tintagel, nine months later. It was a cold starry winter's night, and I stood on the shore where a secret passage from the castle comes out. I was dressed on that occasion as an old beggarman, and I waited for the queen's lady to come down with the new born baby – you."

"Your father had married Igraine soon after Gorlois' death. He wanted you spirited away in the night as soon as you were born, so you could be brought up in safety. He hoped, I know, that he and Igraine would have at least one other son who would be his heir. He felt ashamed of that night when Gorlois was slain."

"I knew, from what I had seen in the stars and from my dreams of the future, that you were to be the great king we all need, and so I was glad to take you somewhere safe to live and grow up. Sir Ector and his wife agreed to bring you up with their son Kay. While you were there I was able to help prepare you for the great tasks of kingship that lay ahead."

"Sir Ector and his wife were kindness and goodness itself," Arthur replied. "But what part did you play? I knew you only as an occasional visitor to Sir Ector's home, but I begin to suspect that you had a bigger part to play."

"I was the first tutor you shared with Kay when you learnt to read and write. I was also the old hermit who used to talk to you and teach you many things when you visited me in the forest. I was never very far away. It was I who arranged for the sword, the magic sword, to be in the churchyard in London when all the great lords and knights tried to pull it out.

"Because of my magic powers I knew what would happen. Through these same powers, I know too that you will be a great king. But this knowledge of the future warns me now, Arthur, that you will be betrayed in the end by your own affections."

The logs threw up a shower of sparks in the dying fire, and the two men sat silent, each lost in his own thoughts. Then Arthur jumped to his feet, startling his white hound. He was smiling grimly.

"I will bring peace to my people. But there is much to do. You'll stay and help me, Merlin?"

"I'll stay as long as I can. As you say, there is much to do." Merlin's voice was shaking.

So the young king retired to bed, dreaming dreams of glory and victory on the battlefield, followed by peace across the land.

Merlin the magician sat until dawn looking into the glowing embers of the fire, and dreamed his own dreams of the future. These were more troubled, and while he saw glory, he also saw bitter sadness surrounding himself and King Arthur.

3

EARLY BATTLES

"Now you are the king," Merlin advised Arthur, "you should be seen more outside London. Ride with your followers throughout the country. Show you are a strong and active ruler."

So Arthur, with many of the knights and lords who had sworn loyalty to him, rode out through many towns and villages. After some months he announced, "Let's rest here for a while. We'll hold a great feast and have a tournament. It is time we celebrated my coronation."

Word spread, and men came from far and wide to celebrate with the young king.

Among those who arrived from the north was King Lot of Lothian and Orkney. He brought his own army of five hundred knights with him. Five other kings, with their armed supporters, also arrived. King Arthur sent out messengers, bidding them welcome and inviting them to the feast. The answer that came back was, "We do not come to feast with you. We have come to kill you."

Arthur and his supporters quickly withdrew into their castle and made rapid preparations to defend themselves. The hostile kings, led by King Lot, thought it would take no time to starve them out, but as the days went by they began to realise they were mistaken.

After two weeks Merlin arrived and slipped through the defence of the besieged castle, using one of his many disguises. "You would be wise to hold peace talks with these kings, Arthur," he said. "King Lot and his friends have a very large army to support them."

"I'll only talk to them if I am wearing a double layer of chain mail. I don't trust King Lot and his friends at all," Arthur replied.

The talks ended in violent arguments, and as Arthur stormed out of the meeting he shouted, "We must fight these men. I shall not give in to them."

Now Merlin advised the six hostile kings, "You should make peace with King Arthur. He will be the greatest king this country has ever known. I have seen it in the stars. You would be wise to fight with him, not against him."

"We waste our time discussing war plans with a star gazer," King Lot retorted. Even when Merlin told them that Arthur was the son of the late King Uther Pendragon, they jeered, saying, "We would rather fight than bow to a young boy as overlord and high king."

Merlin returned to Arthur. "It seems you will have to do battle with them. Keep your magic sword, the one you pulled from the stone, until the fighting is really fierce. Then bring it out and use it. At the right moment it will turn the battle for you."

The two sides fought a long and bloody battle. Arthur was outnumbered and in the thick of the fighting he was knocked from his horse by King Lot. Arthur's friends immediately surrounded him, and as he remounted he drew his magic sword from its scabbard, and the enemy fell to right and left. Before long the hostile army retreated and as Arthur's men followed them across the plain, Merlin advised Arthur to chase them no further.

A council of war followed in Arthur's camp, and it was decided to ask for help from friendly kings across the water, in Brittany and further south in France. Messengers were sent to King Bors and King Ban who crossed the sea as soon as they could with many fighting men and joined ranks with King Arthur.

Meanwhile King Lot encouraged many kings and nobles from the north to join with him. Merlin's spies reported that King Lot had amassed an enormous army led by eleven kings. They had fifty thousand men on horseback and ten thousand foot soldiers.

Two days before the armies met, King Arthur dreamt that a great gale blew down all the castles and towns of King Lot's supporters. Then came a flood and washed away all the ruins left by the wind. All who heard of the dream foretold that Arthur would win a great victory.

Merlin, who knew which way Lot and his army rode, advised King Arthur that he should make a surprise attack in the night. So at midnight Arthur's army crept up and rushed on the enemy as they slept in their tents. As they did so, King Lot's watchmen raised the alarm, shouting, "To arms! To arms! The enemy is here!"

Many men were killed as they fought in the dark, and then King Arthur called back his men. Merlin came and offered more advice.

"The eleven kings still do not have nearly as much information about us as we have about them," he said. "Let's surprise them again in another way. News of King Ban and King Bors' arrival has not yet reached them. I suggest before daylight comes our allies conceal themselves in this wood. When the two armies confront each other in the morning, let the enemy see only part of your strength. They will feel more confident and ride out with less fear. When they are far from their own base and not expecting extra strength on your side, send a signal to King Ban and King Bors who can then ride out of the wood and take them by surprise."

As Merlin predicted, so it happened. King Lot and his friends saw only about twenty thousand men in King Arthur's army and thought they would have an easy victory. They rode with vigour into the trap that had been set for them, and when Arthur gave the signal, King Bors and King Ban led their men out of the wood and into the battle.

Fierce fighting took place, both on horseback and on foot. Many horses were killed, and many men lay dead or wounded on the battlefield. The battle raged for many days.

"Young Arthur's a fine warrior, no doubt about it," was heard on every side. Merlin, as he slipped through Arthur's ranks, smiled when he heard this.

Arthur's enemies did not believe that they could lose against an army led by a young man with so little fighting experience. But Arthur always judged it right when to lead an attack with knights on horseback, when to call in fresh troops, when to regroup and attack again, and when to give chase to a fleeing enemy.

At last a truce was called. Arthur's enemies withdrew their armies back to their own lands in the north.

* * *

During the following months Arthur continued to ride out across the country fighting where necessary, and attracting support to his cause wherever he could. There were some who complained he gave his followers no chance to hunt and enjoy themselves. But Arthur knew that he must take advantage of his early victories. "There will be time enough for hunting, when the kingdom is secure," he told them.

Arthur never knew when to expect Merlin. He came and went from the king's company in his own time and in his own ways. On one cold and frosty February morning, Arthur was told a huntsman had arrived at the castle where he was staying, and had asked to speak to the king.

"My lord," said Sir Bedivere, "he says he comes to seek a gift from you."

King Arthur looked at his visitor, who was wrapped in black sheep-skins over a russet tunic. He wore country boots and was holding a bow and arrow and he carried a pair of wild geese.

"Why should I give you a gift?" he asked.

"Better you should give me a gift than lose great riches," replied the huntsman.

"Who told you this?" Arthur demanded, angry at the man's impertinence.

"Merlin told me," was the answer.

At this, Sir Bedivere burst out laughing. "Don't you know this man? Shame on you, Arthur. It's Merlin himself."

"Oh, Merlin, how can you fool me and everyone else in this way! It must be magic!"

"Magic may play its part in the ways I try to help you, but I can pass as others because I observe people with care. I note their habits, their movements, their expressions, their voices, and in this way I can mimic them and go in many places where it would be difficult to pass as Merlin, the wise man and counsellor to King Arthur."

Whenever he came, Merlin would offer advice to Arthur on when and where to fight, when to hold peace talks and how to extend his rule over much of England. He knew Arthur had to gain many allies as quickly as possible if he was truly to establish himself as high king.

Each year Arthur's support increased. Many of the nobles who at first had resented him becoming king were glad now to declare their loyalty to him. They discovered that Arthur was a king they were proud to serve.

4

THE SWORD IN THE LAKE

Storms had swept across the country for seven days, making it almost impossible for travellers to complete their journeys, but now the sky was clear, the wind had stopped tearing at the trees, and the sun was drying the waterlogged earth. King Arthur stood in his castle tower looking out to the east.

"I wish Merlin would come," he said impatiently. "We have been cooped up here too long waiting for news, yet without reliable information on what our enemies are doing we cannot go out and fight them."

"And you'll never get better information than you do from Merlin," said Bedivere, Arthur's companion. "It is amazing the way he gathers news. But look, I see a group of travellers approaching. Let's go down to the courtyard and wait for them. Perhaps Merlin is among them."

"Riders are coming in from the north, too, my lord," a guard told Arthur. "One looks sorely wounded. His horse is being led by a young squire."

The two horses from the north were the first to arrive. On one a dead man lay across the saddle.

"Who's this?" asked Arthur.

"This is the body of the bold Sir Miles," said the squire. "He was riding to join you, when we came across a fierce and unfriendly knight guarding the road through the valley up there. He would not let us pass, but challenged Sir Miles to a fight. I know of no other man who would have defeated my master, but they fought hard and long, and at the end the stranger wounded Sir Miles so grievously that he died before I could bring him here."

"By thunder, we will have revenge for this," cried Arthur, "for no man in my kingdom should prevent others travelling to see me. Who is this dangerous and unfriendly neighbour?"

Just then the other party of travellers rode in, with Merlin leading the way. "We have visitors from Rome," he told Arthur. "They have travelled far to see you. While they refresh themselves, you can tell me your news, and why a dead knight is lying across a horse in your courtyard."

"This was bold Sir Miles, who was slain by an unfriendly knight who will not let travellers pass down the valley from the north," said Arthur.

Suddenly a young man pushed his way forward. "Let me avenge Sir Miles. I would like to go out and kill this knight now, today!"

"Bravely spoken, Griflet, but you are not even a knight. How will you slay this unknown enemy?"

"Make me a knight now, and I will show you how all the practice we have had at jousting and sword play has taught me how to kill your enemies."

At this Merlin advised Arthur, "You will be wasting a good man if you allow young Griflet to go out and fight the man in the valley. I know about him. He is called Sir Pellinore, and he will kill anyone who challenges him, for he jousts on horseback and fights with a sword better than most. He is older and tougher than Griflet, and is sure to win in any contest between them. Griflet will be a brave knight in the future. It would be wise to keep him alive."

But Griflet begged King Arthur to let him go, and Arthur was angry with Sir Pellinore and wanted revenge.

"I'll make you a knight now, Griflet, but only on one condition."

"I'll promise anything you ask, my lord."

"Promise you will return as soon as you have fought with him, whether on foot or on horseback. Do not challenge him again, even if you lose, for I will need your services in the years to come."

Griflet gave his word and knelt before Arthur in the courtyard. Arthur laid his sword on Griflet's shoulder and said, "Arise, Sir Griflet. Go and avenge Sir Miles."

Sir Griflet scarcely waited to collect his armour before he mounted his horse and galloped full speed towards the valley where Sir Pellinore challenged all who came.

Now King Arthur turned to the twelve men from Rome, who had ridden in with Merlin.

"We come from the emperor to collect your tribute, since we hear you are now the high king of this land. The emperor told us to say that if you do not pay him this money he will come with an army and lay waste your land."

At this Arthur grew red with rage. "You are merely messengers, and I cannot punish you for delivering the message from the emperor. But you can tell him from me, that I pay no man for being high king of England. It is many years since the Roman emperors called back all their men from this land. If the emperor does not accept my answer I will challenge him personally to a fight, either with spear or sword. No man is my master!" and he bade the messengers be gone before they felt the force of his arm.

* * *

Meanwhile Sir Griflet rode up the valley and arrived at a fountain. There he saw a shield hanging from a tree, and beside the path a pavilion or grand tent had been erected. He struck the shield that hung there, and an enormous man appeared in the entrance to the tent.

"Who are you, and why do you strike my shield?"

"I have come from King Arthur's court to fight you, to avenge the death of bold Sir Miles."

"You would be wise to return straightaway to King Arthur, for you are too inexperienced to fight me," replied Sir Pellinore.

"That makes me all the more determined to fight," returned Sir Griflet.

So Sir Pellinore accepted the challenge, put on his armour and rode against Sir Griflet. Within minutes he had broken Sir Griflet's shield, and run his spear through Sir Griflet's armour, wounding him deep in the side. The blow was so violent that Griflet's horse was winded and lay on the ground as though dead. Now Sir Pellinore went to the young knight, and loosened his helmet to help him breathe. As Griflet's horse staggered to its feet, Sir Pellinore placed Sir Griflet across the saddle. "Take your foolhardy young master home," he advised the horse, and he returned to his tent to await the next challenge.

Everyone was aghast to see Sir Griflet return, weak and bleeding, lying across his horse. He was lifted carefully down and the best medical advice was sent for.

Now King Arthur was really angry. "I had been hoping for action today, but this is too much. First the brave Sir Miles is killed, then I am insulted by the messengers from the emperor in Rome, and now Sir Griflet, the bravest young man in the castle, lies sick and may die. I'll send no other man to seek revenge, but go myself. Have the best horse in the stables and all my armour and my special sword ready, for I leave at dawn."

So, at first light Arthur rode out to challenge the knight who would let no man pass. As he rode through the forest he came upon three ruffians attacking one man. He rode at them, shouting that they should stop, and discovered that the man being attacked was none other than Merlin. "I might have guessed you would be ahead of me," he said. "I suppose you thought you would stop Sir Pellinore from fighting me! But you're the one who was in danger. You'd have been dead by now, if I hadn't come along."

"I would have saved myself by magic or some other means," said Merlin, "but you are in far greater danger. I can smell death. It is hanging in the air."

As they argued, they arrived in the clearing by the fountain where Sir Pellinore had pitched his tent. There waiting in front of it was a great knight, armed and ready to fight.

"I have come to tell you that you must stop challenging all those who come this way," said King Arthur.

"Sir," replied the knight, "this is the way I have always behaved, and I see no reason for changing it, whoever bids me do so."

"Then," said Arthur, "I must challenge you. When I have won you will understand who is master around here!"

"I shall defend my right!" said the knight, and he prepared to fight.

The two men faced each other on horseback, each with his shield held before him, and a spear levelled at the other. They rode at speed towards each other, and clashed so hard that both their spears were smashed to smithereens against the other's shield. Arthur's hand went to his sword.

"Not yet," said the knight. Let us joust again with spears."

"I would if I had another with me," replied Arthur.

"I have plenty more," said the knight, and called over a squire who fetched two spears. Once more the two men faced each other, with shield in place, spears levelled. At the same moment they spurred their horses forward, and at full speed clashed together. Once more both their spears were shattered. Sir Pellinore said, "You joust better than any other I have met. Let us meet once more with spears."

Again the squire brought out new spears, and the two men charged at each other. This time Sir Pellinore hit Arthur a terrific blow, breaking Arthur's spear, and knocking him from his horse. Arthur drew his sword and shouted, "Now I will fight you with my sword. You have the better of me with spears, but I am not yet defeated."

"You have not a chance while I remain mounted," replied his enemy. Then he saw Arthur prepare to attack him, and jumped from his horse, so they were evenly matched.

Now the two men fought fiercely with their swords, cutting and thrusting, sparring and parrying, backwards and forwards they went. They battled with each other like two fighting rams, each with his sword blade striking continually at the other. At last Sir Pellinore raised his sword and smashed it down on Arthur's so the blade snapped in two and lay broken on the ground.

"Now yield," said the knight to Arthur, "for you are at my mercy. Admit you are beaten or you shall die!"

"I'll never yield," gasped Arthur, "so you had better kill me."

"That I will," said Sir Pellinore, and he raised his sword to smite the killing blow. At that moment Arthur leaped at him, seizing him round the middle. He was near to throwing him to the ground when Sir Pellinore gathered his strength once more and bore down on

Arthur until he was crushed beneath him. Pulling off Arthur's helmet, he raised his sword once more.

At this, Merlin intervened. "Do not kill this man, for all that you have him at your mercy. By killing him, you will put the whole kingdom in great danger."

"Who is this young man who fights so well?" asked Sir Pellinore.

"It is King Arthur himself," said Merlin.

Sir Pellinore raised his arm once again, for he feared the king's anger if he allowed him to live. But as he did so, Merlin cast a spell on him, and at once Sir Pellinore fell to the ground, unconscious.

"Why ever did you do that? It would have been better for me to die, than live only because you save me by your magic!" Arthur cried.

"Not so, for your destiny is to be a great king. This man will come to no harm. He will recover in a few hours, but you are badly wounded and need caring for if you are to live. It is well done, for you have proved you can fight the finest warrior in your kingdom, and he will serve you well in the future. His sons will serve you too."

Arthur was very weak from his wounds, so Merlin helped him to a cave in the forest where a wise man skilled at healing with herbs, cared for him. For three days Arthur lay there unable to move, but gradually the medicines worked and Arthur was once more strong enough to sit on a horse. As they left the cave, Arthur said, "I may be alive, Merlin, but I no longer have a sword. It will be hard to return home without a sword."

"We are on our way to get a special sword that is waiting for you," said Merlin.

* * *

They rode out of the forest, up a stony mountain track and through a pass into a hidden valley where there was a broad lake surrounded by wild and desolate hills. As they approached it they saw, lit by a beam of brilliant sunshine, an arm coming out of the lake and holding a sword aloft.

"Look!" said Merlin. "There is the sword I spoke about."

Even as Merlin spoke, Arthur saw a strange and beautiful girl walking across the water towards them.

"Who is she? Where has she come from?" asked Arthur, staring at her, wondering if he was dreaming.

"That is the Lady of the Lake."

"Lady," said Arthur, bowing to her as she approached, "whose sword is that? I wish it were mine, for I have no sword."

"That sword is mine. Its name is Excalibur. You shall have it for your use, if you promise to return it to me when you have no more need of it."

"I shall return it as you ask," replied King Arthur, gazing at the sword that glistened and sparkled as it was held above the lake.

"Then go into that boat, and row across the water. When you reach the sword, take it and the scabbard."

So Arthur, with Merlin beside him, rowed out to the middle of the lake, until they reached the arm which was still holding out the sword Excalibur. Arthur leant out of the boat and took the sword, with its scabbard. As he gazed at the jewelled hilt and finely worked metal the hand slipped silently into the water and out of sight.

Now Arthur saw a fine tent standing by the lake which he had not noticed before.

"Whose tent is that?" asked Arthur.

"Sir Pellinore's," was Merlin's answer.

"Then I will fight him," said Arthur quickly, "for I owe him a blow or two for the beating he gave me last week."

"If you take my advice, you shall do no such thing," said Merlin. "That man will be a valuable ally one day, as will his sons, as I have already told you. Be at peace with him."

"I'll do as you say, Merlin," said Arthur.

As he rode he could not help looking at the magnificent sword that now hung from his belt.

"Which do you prefer? The sword, or the scabbard?" asked Merlin.

"I like the sword better," replied Arthur.

"Then you are unwise. Each has magical properties; but the scabbard is worth ten times the sword, for whoever wears it shall never bleed to death however deep his wounds may be. Take care to keep it with you always.''

''I'll take care,'' said Arthur, gazing with wonder again at both the sword and the scabbard.

A group of knights was waiting anxiously at the castle. They were relieved to see King Arthur ride in with Merlin, for they had heard no news for several days and feared he had been killed by Sir Pellinore. Arthur told them of his adventures, and showed them his wonderful new sword.

''Long live King Arthur,'' they shouted as Arthur arranged for a great feast to be held in honour of his safe return with the magic sword Excalibur.

5

THE ROUND TABLE

As the years went by more and more men acknowledged Arthur as their king, but there were still some ready to challenge him. One evening, as Arthur and his companions came in from the jousting field at Camelot, which was now King Arthur's capital, a messenger from King Rience arrived. King Arthur greeted him courteously. The messenger was not so polite.

"My lord, the King Rience sends you this message. Eleven kings have recognised him as their master, and each one of the eleven has sent his beard to trim King Rience's cloak. But there is one place on the cloak which still needs trimming, and he bids me bring your beard. If I return without it he will come with his army and burn and plunder your land, until you agree to acknowledge him as your superior lord."

"By all that's true, your master shall not have my beard, nor my allegiance. Tell him that no man is master of King Arthur. This is my answer to King Rience. Now leave my kingdom at once."

As the messenger rode quickly away from Camelot one of Arthur's men arrived with the news that King Rience and his army was already approaching Arthur's kingdom.

"Prepare for battle!" King Arthur gave the order. "We leave at dawn tomorrow!"

King Arthur's force rode hard, and found a vast army preparing to fight them on the borders of Wales. At its head was King Rience, and lined up to fight with him was King Lot of the Orkneys, Arthur's old enemy and husband of Morgause, Arthur's half-sister. Arthur's band of armed soldiers and knights on horseback was outnumbered,

34

but Arthur knew his men were well trained and would obey him to their last breath. He also knew he had the magic sword Excalibur at his side, and the magic scabbard that would never let him bleed to death.

Just as the battle began, Sir Pellinore arrived, and joined Arthur's side.

"Welcome! Merlin told me I'd be glad of your help one day," King Arthur shouted to Sir Pellinore, as he led the first charge.

As the battle raged backwards and forwards, men were struck down on every side and hand to hand fighting took place across the battlefield. But Arthur regrouped his knights under his banner with the red dragon leaping across it. They charged more than once, forcing the enemy ranks apart. The turning point in the battle came when King Lot, rallying his men against Arthur, came up against the powerful figure of Sir Pellinore. With one massive stroke Sir Pellinore had King Lot on the ground, and had thrust his spear into King Lot's side. Word spread quickly that Lot was dead, and Arthur's victory was soon complete. King Rience and his army fled into the mountains of Wales in a disordered retreat.

"So, my beard is saved!" said King Arthur. "And so, too, is my kingdom!"

On their journey back to Camelot, Arthur and some of his knights spent a few days with King Lodengrance at Camelerd, hunting and feasting. Guinevere, the lovely daughter of King Lodengrance, sat next to Arthur at the high table, and rode out with him when a hunting party went into the forest to chase a stag. He found Guinevere's beauty bewitching and soon he could think of nothing and no one else.

"Merlin," he said, on his return to Camelot, when he had finished telling him of the battle and King Lot's death, "I think it is time I married. I should like to have a wife by my side. And Camelot should have a queen."

"Your decision to marry is a wise one," said Merlin, "for you have passed your twentieth birthday, and your people will soon want to know you have an heir. Would you like me to search for a suitable princess?"

"I have already found her. She is Guinevere, the daughter of King Lodengrance."

Now Merlin was troubled, for he could see a shadow cast over the future of Arthur and Guinevere. But, it was only a shadow, and there was no reasonable objection he could raise. Lodengrance was a good ally, and word of Guinevere's beauty had already come to Merlin. So he said, "If a man's heart is set on one woman, however many other beautiful women there are, his heart is unlikely to change."

"You are right," said Arthur, knowing his heart would never change.

"Then let me ride to Lodengrance, and discuss the matter with him," Merlin suggested. "It will be good to see a queen by your side and a young family here in Camelot."

Lodengrance was delighted. "I can think of nothing better for my daughter," he told Merlin. "Arthur is high king, so it will be a great honour for Guinevere to be his queen, but he is also a handsome young man and brave in battle. He will be most welcome to me as a son-in-law. And surely Guinevere cannot help but love such a man."

As Merlin greeted Guinevere he saw a young lady of radiant beauty, who seemed to be as much struck with Arthur as he was with her. "Why," Merlin asked himself, "why should I be uneasy about this marriage?"

"Tell Arthur," Lodengrance said, "I will give the young couple as a wedding gift the great round table Arthur's father, Uther Pendragon once gave to me. It is big enough to seat one hundred and fifty knights. I have no use for it now, and in Camelot, it will serve for both feasts and councils. What is more, I will send one hundred knights to sit at the table and to add to Arthur's fighting strength."

When Merlin returned to Camelot, he rode with Guinevere beside him on a white horse, which had been a present from Arthur. They were followed by a hundred knights. Behind, with the baggage, followed the huge round table of Uther Pendragon.

Arthur stood at the gates of Camelot and welcomed Guinevere with joy. "Guinevere shall be crowned queen on our wedding day. And on that day we shall all feast at the Round Table," he announced.

The Round Table was rumoured to have magic qualities and Merlin recognised it as a great gift to Arthur. Gone now would be the days of quarrelling as to who was more important, and therefore who sat nearer the top of the long oak table where King Arthur held council meetings. As King Arthur sent out a search for fifty true followers to sit at the table with the hundred knights who had arrived with Guinevere, Merlin joined his magic to that of the table.

On the day before the wedding, Arthur came with Merlin to the great hall where his followers were gathered. Among the visitors was the Archbishop of Canterbury who had come to conduct the service. Now Merlin asked all those knights present to come and give allegiance to Arthur. Each man knelt in turn and vowed loyalty to his king and as he returned to his seat, if his heart was true, he found his name written there in gold letters by Merlin's magic. Sir Bedivere, Sir Kay, Sir Lucan, Sir Griflet and many more names were there for all to see.

There were gasps of wonder and amazement from all the assembled company. "This is magic, indeed," said Arthur, "but tell me why some places remain empty." All eyes looked to Merlin for they knew of his magic powers.

"Some of the knights destined to sit at the Round Table are not yet born," Merlin told Arthur. "Two more will come today, but that seat there will remain empty for many years. It is called The Seat of Danger. It is for one man only and he will come to Camelot when the time is right, and when your kingdom is at its most powerful. He shall be the Perfect Knight."

Towards evening, a young man arrived at Camelot. He had ridden far and was mud-spattered and dusty from the journey, but all could see he was a fine looking youth. He asked to speak with King Arthur. When he was shown to the king he said, "I have travelled far to ask you to make me a knight now, for I would like to sit at the Round Table with your other followers tomorrow. My name is Gawain. I am son of King Lot and Queen Morgause."

"Then, Gawain, you are my nephew for you are my sister's son. I will be glad to have your loyalty." And Arthur took a sword and laid it on Gawain's shoulders, saying, "Arise, Sir Gawain."

The same evening a roughly dressed cowherd came to Camelot and asked to speak to King Arthur. When he was shown to the king he said, "I ask you to make my son a knight. He wishes to sit with your company at the Round Table."

At this, Arthur's advisers said, "You do not want a cowherd's son at your Round Table. It is only for brave knights and men of good families."

"What is his name, and why do you ask this?" Arthur asked the cowherd, for he thought the son looked handsome and likely to be brave in battle.

"His name is Tor. I have thirteen sons, and all are willing to work on the land, except for Tor who wishes to serve you."

"Where is a sword, Tor, so that I may make you a knight?" was Arthur's reply. Tor handed him a sword, and King Arthur touched his shoulders with the blade and said, "Arise, Sir Tor."

Now at the table they all could see the names of both Sir Gawain and Sir Tor written in gold.

As Merlin approached, Arthur said, "Here is Sir Tor, son of this cowherd. Tell me, Merlin, since you can see into the future, will he be a good knight?"

Merlin looked hard at the young man, saw he was different from his brothers and his father, and asked to see the mother. She told Merlin that Tor was not the cowherd's son, but the son of Sir Pellinore. "He loved me when he was a young man, and when he left me with child, he arranged that I should marry this good man here who has tended cows all his life. Pellinore took a deerhound of mine as a keepsake or love token."

"Then," said Merlin to Sir Tor, "your father, Sir Pellinore, is a gallant knight. It was he who bravely killed one of King Arthur's enemies, King Lot, in battle this year. My magician's knowledge tells me that you, too, will become a brave and fearless knight like your father."

The next morning, before the wedding and coronation, Sir Pellinore rode into Camelot. King Arthur gave him a great welcome and took him over to meet his son, Sir Tor. "He is a fine young man. I am proud and pleased to see him after all these years," Sir Pellinore said.

As Arthur showed him the Round Table, he too found his name in gold written at his place.

At the wedding feast, Queen Guinevere sat on the king's right hand. She was dressed in clothes of fine white and gold material, while her jewels, a gift from her husband, sparkled and shone, showing off her beauty. All the men present gazed at her with admiration. King Arthur, too, looked magnificent, with a white tunic and cloak with the red dragon embroidered across the back. At his side hung his magic sword Excalibur, with the hilt and scabbard glinting with jewels.

Arthur looked at the great gathering of men around the table, and stood to make a speech. At that moment a shaft of sunlight came through one of the high windows of the hall, and surrounded him so that he himself seemed ablaze with light. He spoke quietly but with fierce determination.

"I want it to be known far and wide that all those who sit at this Round Table are the finest knights in the world. Your bravery will surpass all others. You will fight the bad, protect the good and always be honourable and true to ladies. Your quests and adventures shall be remembered in years to come. But today, raise your goblets and drink with me a toast to my lovely queen, Guinevere."

"Queen Guinevere! King Arthur!" The knights rose to their feet and shouted till they were hoarse.

6

THE QUEST OF THE WHITE HART

King Arthur stood at the Round Table and listened to the men cheering. It was his wedding day, and Queen Guinevere, his bride, beautiful with her long golden hair and her gown of gold and white, was at his side. As their shouts died down he spoke.

"We who are gathered here today, in this great hall of Camelot shall be known as The Knights of the Round Table. Each time we come together for a great feast we shall not eat until a new quest or adventure has been undertaken by us."

Everyone looked around, wondering what adventure might come when they were already sitting in the great hall. As they waited, Sir Gawain beckoned to his younger brother, Gaheris, who had ridden to Camelot with him, and said quietly, "You see that huge man over there, the one that King Arthur is treating with so much honour? He is Sir Pellinore, the knight who slew our father, King Lot. I swear I will kill him as soon as I can, to avenge the death of our father."

"You shall not do this," replied Gaheris. "I am only a squire now, but when I am a knight I shall be the one to slay him. But we should not disturb this great feast with talk of killing other knights. Listen! Something is happening down the other end of the hall!"

A sudden disturbance had taken place by the great oak doors, and a white hart burst into the hall closely followed by a white hound. The eyes of the hart rolled in terror and its flanks were heaving as it ran the length of the hall, with the white hound just behind it. Then thirty pairs of black hounds in full cry came streaming into the hall after them both. The hart swerved this way and that, as it tried to escape from the white hound's snapping jaws, and from the black

hounds who were so close behind.

In the turmoil a knight, called Abellus, whose seat was only at a side table, was knocked over. Exclaiming loudly, he seized the white hound and ran from the hall with it, while the black hounds kept up their chase after the white hart. After going round the table they all ran out of a side door of the hall.

Now all heads turned as a young lady appeared at the main entrance to the great hall. She was riding a white horse, and she shouted angrily at King Arthur, "Why have you allowed that man to leave with my hound? I demand that you order him back immediately so that he can return the hound to me."

Before King Arthur could do anything, a man on horseback, dressed in black armour, appeared. He seized the lady and dragged her roughly away, ignoring her shrieks and cries.

"Thank goodness that's over," remarked King Arthur as the noise and commotion died down.

At this Merlin came forward. "It is not over. No lady should be taken against her will from the hall where you sit with your knights. This is, indeed, an adventure and a challenge. You should not ignore it."

"Tell me what we should do?" the king asked.

"Send Sir Gawain after the white hart, and ask him to bring it back to this court. Send Sir Tor, the other newly made knight, to retrieve the white hound, and to bring back with him the knight who ran out with the hound, or slay him. And send Sir Pellinore after the lady and the knight who came in and treated her so roughly. Let them prove the worth of knights who sit at the Round Table."

So Arthur called out for Sir Gawain, Sir Tor and Sir Pellinore to set off on these quests, and the wedding feast commenced.

* * *

Young Sir Gawain, who had only been knighted the day before, leapt eagerly on his horse and galloped away, with his brother Gaheris following as his squire. They could hear the black hounds baying as they followed the scent of the white hart, so they knew which

44

direction to take.

They rode so fast that they could soon see the black hounds, which were still following the white hart. A wide river lay ahead, and the hart leapt in and swam to the far bank, with the black hounds still following closely behind. As Sir Gawain spurred his horse into the water a knight on the other side rode out of the trees and shouted, "Stay there, for if you cross the river you will have to fight me!"

"I am on the quest of the white hart, so I cannot turn back. If needs be I must fight you!" returned Sir Gawain as he urged his horse through the swift-flowing river.

And so they fought, Sir Gawain and the strange knight on the river bank. Each raised his shield, levelled his spear and charged towards the other. They rode with such speed and force that they met with a great clash, and the strange knight was knocked off his horse.

"Yield now," called out Sir Gawain.

"Never!" replied his opponent. "We will continue the fight on foot, using our swords."

"Tell me first your name," said Gawain.

"I am Alardin of the Isles," replied the stranger.

So they fought, thrusting and parrying with their swords, while young Gaheris held the horses and watched anxiously, fearful that his brother might die. At last Gawain got past his opponent's guard and Alardin of the Isles lay dead at his feet.

"That was a tremendous blow for a young knight," said his young brother admiringly. "But come on, Gawain, you still have to follow the white hart."

They picked up the trail and followed the white hart until it led them right into the courtyard of a castle. There the hounds had cornered the hart and killed it.

Sir Gawain and Gaheris arrived to see a man stride into the castle court, draw his sword and kill two of the hounds, for he knew that his lady would be beside herself with grief at the death of her pet white hart.

"Those hounds were only doing what they were trained to do," cried Gawain. "Why did you kill them? I shall fight you for this!"

So, for the second time that day Sir Gawain fought and it was a bitter fight. Then the stranger lost his footing, and sprawled at Gawain's feet. He cried for mercy, but Gawain would grant him none, although it was the custom to do so in a fight if someone asked for it.

The lady of the castle had come out, and when she saw her lord on the ground and Gawain's sword raised to kill him, she threw herself on to her husband. She was sure Gawain would never strike if a lady lay in the path of his sword. One second too late, she fell as Gawain's sword flashed through the air towards her husband, and she lay dead.

Now Gawain stood gazing in horror, for not only had he refused mercy to a knight who asked for it, he had slain a lady. The world swam around him, and as his vision cleared he saw the knight still at his feet.

"I'll give you all the mercy you want now," he said in a stunned and stony voice.

"I have no more need to live, now that my lady has been slain by you," replied the knight. "I would rather be dead myself."

But Gawain urged him to ride to Camelot and tell King Arthur all that had taken place.

As Gawain and Gaheris rode out of the castle, four knights came up and challenged them and started to fight, calling out to Gawain that he was a man of double dishonour for not allowing a man mercy when he asked for it, and for killing a lady. So sore pressed were they by their four assailants that both Gawain and Gaheris would have died if four ladies had not come along and begged for their lives. So, they were taken as prisoners to a castle where the ladies tended Gawain's arm which had been badly cut. When they heard that Gawain and Gaheris were sons of King Lot of the Orkneys and Queen Morgause, they said, "Then you are the nephews of King Arthur."

"Yes," replied Gawain, "but I have brought no honour to his court."

The ladies told the men who had fought with Gawain and Gaheris that they had King Arthur's nephews imprisoned, and that they should be freed. It was agreed that Gawain and Gaheris should be sent back to King Arthur's court and that Gawain should tell the King and Queen how he had slain a lady while on his quest.

Both Arthur and Guinevere were shocked and saddened that Gawain should have acted with such dishonour, and Guinevere sent for her ladies and asked them to pass judgment on Gawain. They decided that in future he should always be the champion of all ladies and defend them even at great peril to himself.

* * *

Meanwhile Sir Tor set out on his quest to find the knight called Abellus who had ridden so rudely from the wedding feast at Camelot with the white hound. He had not ridden far through the forest when a dwarf stepped into his path and struck his horse on the head with a great stick.

"What are you doing?" cried Sir Tor. "I must go past for I am on a quest from King Arthur's court."

"Before you pass you must fight those who challenge you from the pavilions over there!" came the reply and Sir Tor saw two grand tents, on either side of the forest road. At this, the dwarf blew on a horn, and a knight came riding from one of the pavilions and challenged Sir Tor to a fight. They raised their lances and rode at each other, and in a short time Sir Tor had the other man at his mercy. When he pleaded to yield, Sir Tor released him, and sent him to Camelot to report to King Arthur on how he had met the knight who was on the quest of the white hound. Then a second knight rode out of the pavilions and challenged Sir Tor. Their lances shattered in pieces as they fought, but again Sir Tor triumphed, and told the defeated knight to ride with his fellow to King Arthur's court, and tell how he, too, had fought and lost against the knight on the quest of the white hound.

"So I will!" he called out, and rode off.

Now the dwarf came and asked Sir Tor a favour. "Let me ride with you as a servant," he begged. "I know you ride after the knight who took the white hound from the great hall of Camelot. I can lead you to him."

"Take a horse, and ride with me, by all means," Sir Tor replied.

In time they came to two pavilions erected outside a priory. Sir Tor dismounted and looked in the first pavilion. There he saw three ladies sleeping. In the second pavilion one lady slept on a couch, with the white hound lying beside her. As soon as it saw Sir Tor it started to bark, and the lady awoke. Sir Tor picked up the dog, and ran off quickly, as the lady called out, "Stop! How dare you take my hound!"

"Lady, I take the hound for I have been instructed by King Arthur to find it and bring it to his court," replied Sir Tor, and he mounted and started to ride off.

"You won't get far," he heard her call after him. "You'll soon be overtaken by a better man than you who will punish you for this."

Darkness was falling and Sir Tor knew they could not ride far, so the dwarf led them to a simple dwelling where a holy man lived. He gave them lodging and a frugal supper for themselves and a shelter and hay for their horses, and in the morning they rode on, taking the white hound with them.

Soon they heard shouting behind them, and a voice calling, "Stop! You there!" It was Abellus, the knight who had run from the great hall in Camelot with the white hound. "Return the hound you took, for it belongs to my lady!"

"I cannot return it," replied Sir Tor, "for I have been bidden by King Arthur to bring it to the court of Camelot, and I was challenged to bring you too!"

"Then we must fight!" cried Abellus, and charged. The fight was fierce, first on horseback, and then on foot with swords. At one time both men paused to loosen their armour as they were badly wounded, but still they fought on, until Abellus was on the ground, and Sir Tor told him to yield.

"Never!" cried Abellus, "while there is breath in my body, unless you hand over my lady's white hound."

As he spoke, a lady mounted on a pony galloped into the clearing where they fought, and asked Sir Tor to grant her a favour.

"Ask for what you will," said Sir Tor, "and if possible I will grant it."

"I ask for the head of that knight Abellus, who is at your feet. He is a murderer, and a false knight."

"I would rather you made your peace with him," said Sir Tor.

"I shall never do that," said the lady, "for he killed my brother, even though I knelt in the mud for half an hour, asking mercy. If you do not kill him now for me, I shall ride out and tell all the world that you are a false knight, for you did not grant me a favour when I asked it. But if you kill him you shall be known as the man who killed the most wicked knight."

At this Abellus cried for mercy, for he could see that Sir Tor was tempted to kill him.

"I cannot grant you mercy now," replied Sir Tor, "without failing in my honour to this lady. I would have granted it to you before, but you would have none of it, only demanding the white hound which I have to take to King Arthur."

When Abellus heard these words, he took off his helmet and turned to flee. In an instant Sir Tor was after him, and with a great swing of his sword, Abellus was dead.

"That was well done," said the lady to Sir Tor. "It will soon be night, so come to my home and spend the evening with my husband and myself, and go on to King Arthur's court tomorrow."

So, three days after he had set out, Sir Tor returned with the white hound and the head of Sir Abellus. All at Camelot were delighted to see him safely returned. He was given many gifts, because he had arrived at court so ill-equipped and had set out on his quest with borrowed things. His father, Sir Pellinore, gave him a horse, and King Arthur presented him with armour and a sword, and on Merlin's advice King Arthur also gave him some land.

* * *

Sir Pellinore's quest was to fetch the lady who had ridden into the hall at Camelot, and had then been taken away by the knight in black armour. As Sir Tor and Sir Gawain set out, he too rode and fast and furiously, determined to catch the two he was following. He galloped so fast through a clearing in the forest where a fountain stood, that he scarcely noticed a young lady. She was seated by the fountain with a wounded knight whose head rested in her lap.

"Help me! I need help!" she called out to Sir Pellinore, but he did not stop. As he disappeared into the distance she cried out in desperation, putting a curse on Sir Pellinore, that he should suffer in the future as much as she was suffering now.

By evening Sir Pellinore had caught up with the lady he was following. She was sitting on her horse and watching as two men fought each other. She told Sir Pellinore that she was Nimue, the Lady of the Lake, and that they were fighting over her.

"Stop your fighting!" Sir Pellinore called out to them, "for I have come to take this lady back to King Arthur's court."

"She shall not go with you," said the knight in black who had ridden away with her, "unless you get off your horse and fight us!" With that, he plunged his sword into Sir Pellinore's horse, killing it.

Sir Pellinore was furious, and drew his sword at once. Within a few minutes the young man was dead. When the other knight saw this, he refused to fight Sir Pellinore, but invited him to his castle, as a guest, before taking the Lady Nimue back to Arthur's court.

The next morning, Sir Pellinore and Nimue set out for Camelot. As they rode they passed the fountain which Sir Pellinore had galloped past as he rode out. There lay two dead bodies, one of the wounded man; the other was the lady who had called out in vain for help.

Now Sir Pellinore wept, for he knew he had done wrong. The young lady's face was strangely familiar, although he did not remember seeing her before.

"We should take the lady's body with us," instructed Nimue. So they rode on to Camelot, carrying her corpse across the front of Sir Pellinore's saddle.

They presented themselves to King Arthur and Queen Guinevere on their arrival, and Guinevere scolded Sir Pellinore for failing to stop when a lady asked for help. "You must remember," said Sir Pellinore, "that I was riding on a quest for you and King Arthur. I was thinking only about what I had to do for you."

Then Merlin joined them, and when he saw the body Sir Pellinore carried with him, he said, "That young woman was your own daughter, although you never knew her. The young man was betrothed to her. He received wounds from a wicked knight, and when he died, your daughter killed herself with his sword. Because you failed her in her hour of need, you too will find your truest friend will fail you when you need him most."

* * *

The adventures of Sir Gawain, Sir Tor and Sir Pellinore, who rode out from Camelot on the wedding day of King Arthur and Queen Guinevere, were often told as storytellers travelled with their harps from castle to castle, town to town and village to village. News spread of King Arthur's court, the finest in the world, where men set out to do brave deeds, to show no cowardice, to give mercy to those who sought it, and to honour and help ladies at all times. These were the Knights of the Round Table who found, when they came to Camelot, their names by magic were written in gold at their places.

7

MERLIN'S TOMB

Arthur, high king, ruler of many parts of England, brilliant in battle, and fierce on the tournament field, had turned to Merlin for advice of every kind since he'd been a boy. Over the last ten years Merlin, by reading the stars and seeing pictures in the flames of flickering fires had seen into the future and advised the young king when to fight and when to make peace with his enemies. It was Merlin who had helped Arthur to build the great city of Camelot and it was through Merlin's magic that the name of each knight was written in golden letters at his seat at the Round Table before he took his place there. Merlin, too, had led Arthur to the lake where he found the magic sword Excalibur. Nimue, the Lady of the Lake, was now in Camelot and the constant companion of Merlin.

Merlin, who was now frail and failing in strength, seemed only to think of the Lady Nimue. When Arthur tried to talk to him about her, the older man shook his head and told Arthur that he had once had a grim glimpse into his own future. "It seems that I am destined to be buried alive. This I fear more than living until I'm so old that I become useless and childlike. But before I go I must pass on some of my knowledge and my skills to another. You have need of a friend at Camelot who is trained in the magic arts. Your two sisters, Morgause and Morgan know enough of evil magic to do you great harm. The Lady Nimue will be by your side and advise you after I am gone. It was a good day for us all when Sir Pellinore brought her back to Camelot in his part of the Quest of the White Hart."

Merlin and Nimue often disappeared from Camelot for weeks at a time. Some said they travelled to Brittany, or even deeper south into

France while others spoke of their being seen in the hidden valleys of Wales, or in the mists and mountains of the far north, or across the sea in Ireland. With Merlin everything was always shrouded in mystery.

On their last visit to Camelot, King Arthur talked to Merlin, trying to make him return to his life at court. "You are a great magician, Merlin. Can you not change the future, so you never have to leave us? Surely you can make some enchantment to prevent yourself from going to your tomb while you still live."

"I would that I could," Merlin replied, "but even my magic is not strong enough for that kind of enchantment. But I must warn you, Arthur, to guard your sword Excalibur, and the scabbard that came with it, with the greatest care, for I can see that they will be stolen from you by a woman whom you do not think of as an enemy. Trust no woman."

"Why should any woman want my sword?" said Arthur.

Merlin ignored the interruption and continued. "Your court, here at Camelot, will increase in glory until all the seats at the Round Table are filled. More knights are yet to come, whose names will live on with yours far into the future. Sir Lancelot, Sir Tristan, Sir Percival, are names that will bring great fame and honour to the Knights of the Round Table, but one of these will bring sorrow too. There is yet another, still not born, and whose name I do not see clearly. He will be the Perfect Knight. When he comes to Camelot, his seat will be the one that is called the Seat of Danger."

"How will I know him?" Arthur asked.

"When he comes to Camelot, you will know him," Merlin replied.

"Merlin, please don't leave us," Arthur urged, for he sensed this might be the last time he would ever talk with his old friend, teacher and counsellor. "How can I face the perils you speak of without you at my side?"

"I have to go," Merlin said, his eyes misting over for he knew he would never again talk with Arthur, the boy he had raised to be high king. "But remember, there is a prophecy that you and I will both come again to Britain when we are needed. This may be why I shall lie in my tomb for hundreds, maybe thousands of years, sleeping but not dead. I shall not be with you when you fight your last great battle but you will never really die. You will be taken when you are near death to an island called Avalon, where you will stay until you are called to return to this land we both love. I know too, Arthur, that no man will ever see you dead.''

At first light the following morning Merlin departed from Camelot with the Lady Nimue. Reports came to Arthur, saying they had been seen in one place and then another, travelling always on and on, with a restless frenzy, until no further word came. Merlin had slipped away to a place where he could no longer be reached.

* * *

On this last journey, Merlin knew he should pass on to his companion all the wisdom and magic that still remained with him. They avoided towns and villages, for Merlin was sure that people watched for him and sent messages back to Camelot. They had crossed the sea once more, and were in King Ban's kingdom. Merlin and the Lady Nimue sheltered at night in caves or deserted barns and empty farm buildings. Merlin stayed close to the fire they made each evening, for the cold crept into his bones, and he would talk far into the night while Nimue listened and learned from the old man. The wisdom he taught her was the knowledge of the ancient people, who had lived in Britain since the beginning of man, long before the Romans or other invaders crossed the seas. It was the wisdom of the little dark people, the people of the hills.

"We have one last visit to make," said Merlin, one morning, as they washed in a spring and ate some dry bread with honey from the wild bees. "We are near the home of King Ban. I wish to talk to his son, Lancelot, before I go to my long rest."

The Lady Nimue, knowing how strange they must look, led Merlin, who was now an old man with shuffling steps, long hair, unkempt beard and shabby clothes, towards King Ban's castle. They were challenged as they approached, but Merlin requested in a shaky voice that they be admitted to the king and queen. As the guard hesitated, he saw the brilliant burning eyes of the old man, and without another word he led the strange pair to his master.

It was many years since King Ban had seen Merlin, but he quickly recognised him and gave him a warm welcome. Merlin presented the Lady Nimue to King Ban and his queen and asked them to call their son, Lancelot.

Lancelot, a youth of seventeen, came at his father's summons. ''You must go to King Arthur's court,'' Merlin said to the young man. ''Ride to Camelot next Easter and present yourself. King Arthur will make you a knight. A place awaits you at the Round Table. Tell King Arthur it was I, Merlin, who sent you. Tell him I came to see you on my last journey.''

''Will he accept me at the Round Table when I'm still so young?'' asked Lancelot.

''He will accept you,'' said Nimue, replying instead of Merlin. ''Tell the high king you come from us, and tell him that I, known by many as the Lady of the Lake, say that once you become a knight you shall be called Sir Lancelot of the Lake.''

Merlin and Nimue ate that day at King Ban's home, and then continued on their travels. It was late in the month of May when they set out from there and took a boat to return to England. Larks sang high above them as they walked along the ancient tracks of Cornwall and towards the hills of Wales. They passed none but the occasional shepherd. ''Less than a moon's cycle now before the longest day,'' said Merlin, ''and by then I will be gone.''

The hawthorn blossom has a heady musky scent, more bitter than many blossoms. This year the hawthorn trees were especially heavy with flowers, some deep red, some white and some a delicate pink. Everywhere Merlin and Nimue went on that last walk, the scent of hawthorn went with them. It blotted out the more gentle aromas from herbs, and fragrances from other blossoms and wild flowers, until it seemed to seep into all their senses, and affect their very thoughts.

Merlin sought a hillside where an ancient, gnarled hawthorn tree stood by a high boulder. One evening near midsummer they came at last to the place. Before the boulder was an area of grass so smooth that it might have been mown for them. A great tangle of wild roses sheltered them from the east wind. A pool of water, fed by a spring that came from where the boulder and the rose bushes met, provided them with a welcome drink.

Nimue spread out her cloak, and Merlin lay down, weakened by the climb.

"Have you been here before?" she asked.

"Many thousands of years ago," was his only reply, as he closed his eyes and seemed to drift into sleep. The hawthorn tree, white in reality, but pink now from the reflection of a flaming sunset, stood over them like a flaming torch.

Nimue took out the small harp they always carried with them on their travels, and started to play. Merlin laid his head in her lap. With his eyes still shut, he lay so still she wondered if he still breathed. But she played on, singing as she played, caught up in a magic greater than her own, greater even than Merlin's.

Afterwards Nimue could only remember sitting by the boulder with Merlin's head in her lap, and singing. The rest of the night seemed hazy and indistinct. Did she dream it, or did it happen, that as she played, the boulder moved to one side, revealing a flight of steps that went down deep into the hillside? If so, she wondered that Merlin had the strength to rise to his feet and go past the boulder and walk down them – down, away from the earth, to his tomb.

Certainly, when Nimue awoke in the chill of the dawn, Merlin was no longer with her. She beat on the boulder with her bare hands, crying out that it should move again so that she could join him. Her tears fell onto the grass, mingling with the dew. She was alone on the hillside, alone with her harp, her dreams, her memories and her magic. Merlin was with her no more.

8

THE MAGIC OF MORGAN LE FAY

"I hear there is a magnificent stag in the forest. We'll go hunting tomorrow," King Urience said to his brother-in-law, King Arthur. "We should have good sport, for the forester tells me he is the biggest beast he has ever seen."

King Arthur and some of the Knights of the Round Table were on a visit to King Urience and his wife Morgan le Fay, Arthur's sister, in North Wales. Merlin had warned Arthur about Morgan and her evil schemes and witchlike ways, but Arthur admired his beautiful sister and he enjoyed the company of King Urience so Merlin's warnings went unheeded.

It was an autumn day of sharp light and brilliant colours when King Urience and King Arthur, in a party of twenty horsemen, rode out into the forest in search of the stag. Among them rode Sir Accolan, a fierce and favourite follower of King Arthur, who was also a secret admirer of Morgan le Fay. The hounds soon found the scent, and the hunting party gave chase. They could see the stag with its great head of antlers running ahead of them, fleeing faster than their horses could gallop. More and more of the hunting party dropped behind but still the hounds clung to the scent, and still the strongest, swiftest horses and the boldest of the riders kept behind them. They crashed through undergrowth, galloped through glades, jumped ditches, scrambled up banks and swam a swift and turbulent mountain river, led always by the stag.

Onward and ever onward they went until only three riders still followed. These were Sir Accolan, King Arthur and King Urience. Yet one by one even their horses foundered, and fell beneath their riders, dead from exhaustion.

"We can't stop now," called King Arthur. "We must follow on foot." They could hear the hounds baying just over the brow of the hill, and they knew they were closing in for the kill. They staggered on foot towards the sound, and found themselves near the sea, overlooking a small sheltered bay. The stag lay on the shore, gasping its last few breaths. As they reached it, it shuddered and died.

The three men stood there, exhausted too. "We have left the others far behind, and we are a long way from home and without horses. What shall we do?" wondered King Urience.

Then they noticed a ship pulled up on the beach.

"Perhaps we can sleep the night on this ship," King Arthur suggested.

It was almost as if they were expected, for suddenly the ship was ablaze with flared lights, and twelve beautiful maidens came out to welcome them, greeting King Arthur by name. On board they found a table laden with food and drink. Suddenly they realised how hungry they were, and as they ate Arthur said he could never remember having a better meal. Then each man was led to a room on the ship that was sumptuously fitted out with comfortable beds, silk hangings and silk cushions, and soon all three were in deep sleep. While they slept the ship sailed out of the bay so quietly they did not even hear the gentle slapping of the water against its sides.

* * *

When King Urience awoke he found himself in Camelot, two days journey from where they had boarded the ship. His wife Morgan le Fay was in his arms. He only had a hazy recollection of the hunt and how he and King Arthur and Sir Accolan had boarded the ship. Knowing his wife had magic powers, he suspected she was involved and thought it best to ask few questions.

* * *

King Arthur, when he awoke, found himself in a dark prison. The

only sound was of other prisoners, groaning and complaining of their plight.

"Who are you and why are we all here?" Arthur called out to them.

"We are all brave knights who have been imprisoned in this castle, some of us for more than seven years," a voice in the dark answered. "The castle belongs to Sir Damas who is a wicked and dishonourable knight. For many years he has been holding lands that belong to his honest brother Sir Onzlake, who has offered to fight Sir Damas to prove his ownership of the land. But Sir Damas is too much of a coward to accept his challenge. He seeks someone who would fight on his behalf, but no knight of honour will fight for him. What is more, Sir Damas is frightened that other knights will challenge him because of the way he has treated his brother, so he sets ambushes for any knight who passes close to this castle. He throws them into this miserable prison before he can be challenged. Many of us have lain here, chained up, for years, and as many have died here in this prison."

"I'd like to save you all," said King Arthur, full of rage that such a man as Sir Damas could live.

A young lady came with a light to the prison and greeted King Arthur. "How are you today, my lord?"

"I can't say I am in good heart," replied King Arthur, "for it does not please me to lie here in prison away from my friends, deprived of my armour and my sword."

"I have a message from the owner of this castle," said the maiden. "He challenges you to a fight. If you refuse, you shall lie here until you die."

"I'll fight your lord," replied King Arthur, "but only on condition that he releases all my fellow prisoners here before I fight."

"That he will do," replied the girl.

"I shall need a horse and my own armour, too, if I am to fight," said Arthur.

"You shall have whatever you require," she told him.

There was something strangely familiar about her, so as she was leaving the prison, King Arthur asked, "I feel I know you. Are you not one of the ladies of my court?"

"I have never been to Camelot," she told him. "My father is the lord of this castle. This is my home." But she was not telling the truth for she was one of Morgan le Fay's ladies whom Arthur had seen at King Urience's court.

* * *

Sir Accolan, when he awoke, found himself beside a deep well. He was lying so close to the edge that he could not move without being in danger of falling down the well shaft. "Now I know we've been betrayed," he said bitterly. "All three of us, King Arthur, King Urience, and myself, have been tricked. We were led to that ship by treachery. If I come out of this adventure alive I shall find those maidens on the ship and punish them for putting us under their enchantment."

As he lay there a dwarf, ugly-faced and flat-nosed, approached, and greeted him, saying he came from his mistress Morgan le Fay. "She bids you be of good cheer, for tomorrow you will fight one of the finest knights in the world. To help you win she has sent you King Arthur's sword Excalibur, and its magic scabbard. When you win the contest you are to ride with all haste to Camelot where you will find Morgan le Fay. Her husband will be dead, and she will already be queen. She will wed you, and together you will rule this land."

Sir Accolan took heart at the dwarf's words and sent a message back to Morgan le Fay, saying he would fight as she asked him, and die for her if necessary. "I think she has made all these enchantments and magic so that we may be together," he said to the dwarf.

"That is so," replied the dwarf. "I will bring you a horse, and you shall ride to a manor near here and rest there before your fight tomorrow." So Sir Accolan found himself staying in the house owned by Sir Onzlake.

Meanwhile Sir Onzlake had received a message from his brother, bidding him to fight the next day, or to send someone to fight in his place.

"I have a slow-healing wound in my thigh. I could have fought with my brother any time in the past few years. Now I'll have to send another to fight for me tomorrow," said Sir Onzlake.

Morgan le Fay's scheme was that Sir Accolan should offer to fight in Sir Onzlake's place. The plan worked for Sir Accolan willingly agreed to go and fight on Sir Onzlake's behalf, confident he would win any contest with King Arthur's magic sword Excalibur in his hand.

So, the next morning, King Arthur rode out believing that he was to fight the wicked Sir Damas, and Sir Accolan rode out, also believing that he was to fight the wicked Sir Damas. Both arrived with their helmets already down over their faces and with no badge on their shields.

The two horses faced each other, the two knights levelled their spears and charged. Neither was unseated at the first impact and they charged again and again. King Arthur was surprised at how good his opponent was, while Sir Accolan, one of the best fighters at King Arthur's court thought, "The only other knight that I know who fights so well is King Arthur himself." Then they came together with such a great clash that both men and both horses fell to the ground. Each man pulled his sword from his scabbard, and they began to fight on foot.

Both men were brilliant swordsmen and their sword blades flashed and sparked as metal hit metal. Both men received wounds, but the strange thing was that while King Arthur lost much blood from the cuts he received, Sir Accolan scarcely seemed to bleed at all. King Arthur, even as he fought, began to suspect treachery for he knew that his magic scabbard that came with the sword Excalibur should prevent him from bleeding to death. He remembered Merlin telling him this.

While these thoughts were going through his mind, Arthur attacked Sir Accolan so fiercely that his sword broke across the top of the blade, and the broken piece fell onto the grass. He was left with only the sword hilt in his hand. Fearful now that he would soon die, he bravely held up his shield and continued to fight unarmed.

Sir Accolan, thinking his enemy was at his mercy, paused and said,

"Strange knight, yield now and admit defeat, or I shall kill you."

"I have sworn on my honour to fight to the end, so I shall continue until there is no breath in my body," replied King Arthur.

At once Sir Accolan attacked again striking King Arthur with a massive blow, King Arthur held up his shield and forced himself against Sir Accolan, hitting him with the broken sword hilt. Sir Accolan reeled backwards, lost his footing and the sword Excalibur fell from his hand.

King Arthur seized it, and knew at that instant that he now held his own sword. "My friend, what damage you have inflicted on me today," he said. Then he spied his own scabbard hanging from his opponent's belt. He grasped it firmly, pulled it away and flung it across the field. Turning to the knight he said, "You have caused great harm with this sword, but now you yourself will suffer for it," and he hit Sir Accolan a massive blow across his head.

"Now I will kill you," said King Arthur, and raised his sword again.

"Slay me if you will, for I promised to battle to the end against an evil knight, but I have to tell you that you are the finest knight I ever fought against."

As he spoke Arthur began to recognise his voice, and said, "Tell me, strange knight, before I kill you, who you are."

"I am Sir Accolan of Gaul. I am from the court of King Arthur."

In a flash King Arthur thought of his sister Morgan le Fay and of her magic, he remembered how the great stag had led them to the ship, and how they had all gone on board and eaten and drunk with the beautiful maidens. He thought of how his sword had been changed so his opponent fought him with it. "Tell me, Sir Accolan," he said in a cracked and shattered voice, "tell me how you came by this sword."

"It was sent to me by Morgan le Fay, sister to King Arthur. She hates and fears her brother more than any man in this world, and has planned to kill him and her own husband Sir Urience. She intends to marry me and together we will rule this kingdom. But I fear the plan has gone badly wrong, for the sword that she stole from the king has dealt me my death blow."

"If you had become king in this way, you would have done great wrong," replied the king.

"I know it," replied Sir Accolan, "and I regret now that I even thought of it. But I have been truthful with you. Tell me now who you are."

"Oh, Accolan, I have to tell you that I am none other than Arthur, your true king."

Now Accolan cried out and asked King Arthur to forgive him. "I did not recognise you, I would not have hurt you."

"I give you mercy," replied King Arthur, "but you are a traitor, for you had planned to kill me. But I know you were under the spell of my evil sister Morgan. She is the wicked mind behind this plot. Merlin warned me against her, but I did not believe my own sister would wish me harm, for I never would have hurt her."

Then Sir Accolan called out to all who were watching the fight, that his opponent was none other than Arthur, their high king. The spectators went on their knees before King Arthur and asked for mercy too.

"We are both badly wounded," King Arthur said. "Let us go and tend our wounds, or neither of us will live. As for you, Sir Damas, you are the cause of this fight, and I will deal severely with you, for you are a man of dishonour. You will hand over all your lands to your brother Sir Onzlake, and you will set free all your prisoners. If I ever hear of your harming these men again, or capturing more knights, then you shall die."

It was too far to ride to Camelot, so King Arthur and Sir Accolan were taken to an abbey where their wounds could be treated. King Arthur made a slow recovery, but four days after the fight Sir Accolan died. King Arthur sent a message to Camelot. "Tell my sister, Morgan le Fay," he said, "that Sir Accolan is dead, and that I have my own sword Excalibur back with me."

* * *

Morgan le Fay, at Camelot, waited until she was sure King Arthur must be dead, and then decided it was time to kill her husband King Urience. As he lay asleep she sent her maid to fetch her husband's sword. But the maid, suspecting her mistress had some evil plan, woke Sir Uwain, son of Morgan and King Urience, and told him, "Go quickly to your mother, for I fear she plans to slay your father. She has sent me to fetch his sword."

"Go and do as my mother bids," said Sir Uwain. "Do not mention you have talked to me, but do not fear, I will come."

While the maid fetched his father's sword, Sir Uwain slipped into his father's room, and hid. He saw the maid bring the sword, and watched as his mother pulled it from its scabbard and stood looking at her husband, wondering which part of his body to strike. As she raised the sword Uwain leapt from his hiding place and held her arm. "What fiend are you to do this?" he cried. "They say that Merlin had magic arts that belonged to the devil, but I would say my own mother is a she-devil in the flesh."

"Have mercy, have mercy," she said. "I will never attempt anything so wicked again."

With this promise, Sir Uwain released his mother.

When the news came to Camelot that King Arthur had regained his sword Excalibur, and that Sir Accolan had died, Morgan hid her grief, for she did not want to be suspected of her part in the tragedy and held against her will in Camelot. Now she went to Guinevere and told her she was going to ride out for she had some business to attend to, and Guinevere said, "No, stay, Morgan, for Arthur will come soon for he has nearly recovered from this wounds. You should wait here for him." But Morgan pressed Guinevere to let her go, and the queen answered, "If you need to go, then go. No one will keep you here."

Morgan rode quickly to the abbey where Arthur still stayed. The monks had instructions not to let any visitors in, but Morgan le Fay wheedled and persuaded, saying, "I come to see my brother, who loves me dearly. You should let me in to his room, even when no other person is allowed." So powerful was her persuasion that they admitted her to the king's room where he lay asleep. The sword Excalibur was in his hand, and she dared not remove it for fear of wakening him. If Arthur saw her now, she knew she would not live. But the scabbard lay propped up against the wall. Swiftly she took it and, hiding it beneath her cloak, she slipped out of the room. She thanked the monks for their help, and rode away as swiftly as she could.

The instant Arthur awoke he noticed his scabbard was missing. "Who has been in here?" he asked.

"None but your sister who rode far to see you. When she saw you asleep she did not waken you," the holy men told him.

"You have guarded me falsely. My sister is the very enemy I feared," he cried, angry that he had been tricked again.

"Sir, we did not think we could refuse your sister's wishes."

"Call Sir Onzlake and saddle two horses. We will ride after her immediately," King Arthur instructed. "She cannot be far ahead."

A cowherd directed them and King Arthur and Sir Onzlake rode as fast as they could. Eventually they caught sight of Morgan le Fay and a company of horses. Giving chase they galloped far through the forest, and out on to a plain.

When Morgan realised she could not escape from her brother, she decided whatever happened she would not let him have the scabbard with its magic properties. A lake lay ahead of them, and so she threw the scabbard as far as she could. It flew through the air and landed deep in the middle of the lake where it instantly sank, for it was heavy with jewels and gold.

She turned herself and her party into great rocks and boulders, so that as King Arthur rode towards the lake he did not see them. He had seen the scabbard fly into the water, though. He and Sir Onzlake spent some time trying to retrieve it, but it had sunk too deep. At last, exhausted, they returned to the abbey. Once they were out of sight, Morgan le Fay restored her party to their normal selves, and they rode on.

* * *

When the king had returned to Camelot, he swore he would punish his sister, and let it be known to everyone that she was never to come to court again. One evening when they were all gathered in the great hall for a feast, a lady arrived and came in to the hall, carrying a long

and beautiful cloak.

"I have a gift for King Arthur," she said. "It is from his sister, Morgan le Fay, who wishes the king to know she is sorry for all the harm and trouble she has caused."

King Arthur did not like this enmity between himself and his sister, and would have been glad to make friends with her again. But as he stretched out for the cloak, Nimue, the Lady of the Lake, put out her hand. She remembered Merlin's warnings.

"Let the lady who brings the gift wear it first," she advised.

"It is not for me to wear a royal cloak," said the messenger. "I have instructions that no one but the high king Arthur, should wear it."

"The Lady Nimue speaks wisely," said the king. "It is my wish that you, my sister's messenger, should show us the true beauty of the cloak by wearing it now for us all to see."

At these words the lady put the cloak around her shoulders. In a flash she was a pillar of flame, and within seconds she was dead.

"Once more I see how much my sister really loves me," said King Arthur bitterly. "But for Nimue's wisdom I would have been burnt to death."

King Urience was excluded from Arthur's anger, for Sir Accolan had told Arthur how he too was to be killed by Morgan le Fay. But Sir Uwain, their son, was banished from Camelot for a time, lest he be part of his mother's evil and magic plans. Sadly Sir Uwain rode out of court. He was followed by his cousin Sir Gawain, who did not think Sir Uwain should bear the blame of this mother's evil deeds.

"Now you have lost two good knights," said Sir Gaheris, Gawain's brother.

"And I have lost my magic scabbard," said King Arthur. "Merlin was right to warn me of the wickedness of some woman that I trusted."

9

SIR LANCELOT OF THE LAKE

As King Arthur and his Knights of the Round Table gathered for their Easter high feast, the year after Merlin had gone into his tomb, three young men rode into Camelot. The leader was a jaunty young man with a self-assured presence. "We have come to see King Arthur," he said to the men at the door of the great hall.

"The King is already at the Round Table," came the reply. " We cannot interrupt him when he is feasting."

"Tell him I come on the instructions of Merlin," the young man said.

They were instantly admitted and all heads turned as the new-comers strode up the hall and the leader knelt before King Arthur and Queen Guinevere. "My lord, my lady," he said, "I am the son of King Ban and Queen Elaine, Merlin came to my father's court last year, and told me it was his last request that I should come to Camelot this Easter and present myself to you. A place awaits me, he said, at your famous Round Table."

"If it was Merlin's wish, then it is mine too. But tell me your name, young man," said King Arthur.

"My name is Lancelot. The Lady Nimue, whom some call The Lady of the Lake, came with Merlin. She told me I should be called Lancelot of the Lake."

"Welcome to Camelot, Lancelot of the Lake! I shall make you a knight tomorrow. I see you have companions. Perhaps they should be knighted too."

"May I present my cousin Lionel, and my half-brother Hector," said Lancelot, as the the two young men in turn knelt before the king. Lionel said he had come to Camelot only to act as Lancelot's squire. "I could not allow anyone else to prepare Lancelot for knighthood," he told the king.

But King Arthur replied, "In three days time, when Lancelot is a knight, you two shall both be made knights also."

There were some at the court, particularly Arthur's foster brother, Sir Kay, who thought these men were too young and unknown to be Knights of the Round Table, and there were murmurs of complaint. But King Arthur refused to listen for Sir Lancelot, Sir Lionel and Sir Hector's names all appeared in gold at the Round Table. Sir Lancelot's was written in the place next to the Seat of Danger. Besides, all three were fine men-at-arms, skilful with sword and spear and good horsemen. Sir Lancelot, particularly, was noticed for the speed with which he could unhorse any opponent in a jousting contest.

Sir Lancelot drew attention to himself, too, for the time he spent with Queen Guinevere. Often they were seen talking, or playing chess together, and she regularly came to watch him on the jousting field. Only one man did not appear to notice this close friendship, and that was King Arthur, who delighted in Lancelot's company -- calling him the finest knight at Camelot. Rumours about Lancelot and Guinevere continued to spread, and these whispers made Lancelot sad. He knew there was truth in what his fellow knights said, for he had fallen in love with Queen Guinevere.

After the feast at Whitsun, Lancelot thought it would be wise to remove himself from Camelot. Perhaps away from the queen he could forget her, or she would forget him. "Come, Lionel," he called out. "Let's ride out on a quest. Let's find some adventures elsewhere in Arthur's kingdom." So they saddled their horses and rode out of Camelot.

It was near midsummer and the June sunshine was scorching hot. By midday they had ridden far, so they hobbled their horses and the two young men ate their lunch under the shade of an apple tree. Then Lancelot stretched out in the cool grass and fell into a deep sleep.

Lionel, more wakeful, sat with his back to the trunk of the tree, looking down the road. To his surprise three knights came galloping

past, hotly pursued by a huge knight on an enormous war horse. Before Sir Lionel's eyes he attacked each of the three knights, knocking them from their horses, and then tied each knight by the wrists and ankles and slung him across the saddle of his own horse. Driving the three horses before him, he rode on.

"Here is a great chance for me to show what a fine knight I am," thought Sir Lionel. "While Lancelot, who normally attracts all the praise and glory, lies here snoozing, I shall go and challenge that wicked knight who has just taken three men prisoner." So, leaving his cousin asleep in the shade, he rode after the huge knight.

"Wait there!" he called out. "I challenge you, for you have taken three men prisoner for no reason that I can see!"

As he raised his lance and started to charge, the great bully of a knight he had challenged, turned and rode at him. In an instant, Sir Lionel was sprawling on the ground. Then he too was bound hand and foot and placed across his own saddle like a sack of flour, and his horse was driven along with the others. Before long all four were thrown into a prison with twenty other knights.

All this time, Lancelot still slept under the apple tree. As the afternoon wore on Queen Morgan le Fay, the king's sister, renowned for her evil enchantments, came along the road with three companions. Each lady rode on a white mule, and four attendants rode with them, carrying a silk canopy held up by four spears, so that the queen and her ladies should not get burnt by the midsummer sun. Lancelot's horse whinnied loudly when it heard the mules and horses passing by.

"What have we here?" asked Morgan le Fay. "A handsome knight asleep under an apple tree." Each of the ladies claimed him for her lover, for they could see how attractive he was.

"I believe he is Sir Lancelot, the darling of King Arthur's court," said one.

"Then let us take him prisoner," said Morgan le Fay, delighted at the thought of making mischief in Arthur's court. She cast a spell on Sir Lancelot, to make him sleep even more deeply, and he was carried back to the home of Morgan le Fay.

On awakening, Lancelot saw he was a prisoner in a castle, and cursed himself for sleeping so soundly. Yet he wondered, as he lay there, why Lionel had not alerted him to danger. A young girl came in, bringing food and drink, and told him he was in the home of Morgan le Fay. Soon he was visited by all of the ladies and Morgan le Fay spoke for them all.

"Welcome, Sir Lancelot of the Lake! What a fine knight you are to be found sleeping unguarded under an apple tree! But you are fortunate, for now you may choose any one of us lovely ladies."

"I choose none of you!" replied Sir Lancelot. "I would rather die first!"

"Ah, he is thinking of his love of Queen Guinevere," taunted Morgan le Fay. "But you will never have another chance to love her, for if you don't choose one of us, you will die here in this castle."

"As for Queen Guinevere, she is loyal only to King Arthur," replied Lancelot, "and if you let me out of here I will ride to Camelot and prove it."

"We will leave you here, until you decide to choose one of us," replied Morgan le Fay.

That evening, Elaine, the girl who brought food and drink to Lancelot, said, "I will let you out of this prison if you will fight for my father in a tournament. My father is King Bagdemagus who was recently defeated in a tournament by some of King Arthur's knights."

"If you will let me out of here, I will gladly fight for your father and help you in any other way I can," replied Lancelot. "But I shall need my horse and my armour."

Elaine came to Lancelot after she had drugged the guards and taken the keys. She led him through twelve locked gates until they both stood outside the castle and Lancelot's horse and armour were there for him. "Ride to a nearby abbey," she told him, "and wait there a few days and I will send word as to how to find my father."

* * *

While Lancelot was in the evil clutches of Morgan le Fay, young Sir Hector noticed Sir Lancelot and Sir Lionel were both absent from

73

Camelot. Afraid he might be missing some good sport he rode out in search of them. On meeting a forester he asked where he might find the best adventures, for he was sure that wherever the action was, that was where he would find his cousin and his brother.

"Ride on this way, young sir," said the forester, "until you come to a manor house near the river. There is a ford where you can water your horse, and by the ford you will see a great copper bowl hanging from a tree with the shields of many knights. Strike the copper bowl with your spear and you will find adventure."

Sir Hector did as he was bid and finding the ford by the manor house and the shields and copper bowl, he struck the bowl hard, and called out, "Whoever lives here, I challenge you to a fight!"

At this, a huge knight rode out and hailed Sir Hector. "If it's a fight you want, you have got it, you young cockerel!" And with no more ado, he charged Sir Hector. But Hector was ready for him and rebuffed him. "Don't think you can get the better of me," cried the huge knight, charging again. Before long, Hector was on the ground. "I like your spirit," said the large knight, "so I'll spare your life. You can go and join my other prisoners."

So Hector found himself imprisoned with his cousin Lionel and others, many of whom were Knights of the Round Table. "Where is Lancelot?" he asked, peering into the gloom of the prison.

"I left him asleep under a tree," said Sir Lionel. "When I heard the prison door opening just now I feared he too had been captured. We must hope he will come this way and rescue us."

Sir Lancelot, though, was many miles away, preparing to help King Bagdemagus win his tournament. Many of the Knights of the Round Table were due to fight in it, so Sir Lancelot decided not to wear a badge on his shield so no one would recognise him. The day of the tournament came and knights from far and wide arrived. One after the other they were defeated by the strange knight who wore no badge and was fighting on behalf of King Bagdemagus. All acknowledged he was the finest fighter any of them had yet encountered.

At the end of the day Sir Lancelot rode away in search of new adventure. So keen he was to be gone before he was recognised, that he did not see Elaine, the girl who had helped him escape from Morgan le Fay's evil clutches, weep as she saw him depart. His own thoughts were still full of Queen Guinevere. Knowing he should not love her for she was wife to King Arthur, he seemed to love her all the more. He knew well that if their secret were known by the king, Guinevere's punishment would be death.

Lancelot rode for many weeks through the forests and plains, seeking shelter where he could and finding adventures along the way. As the nights began to grow cold and the leaves were tinged with gold and scarlet, he came to the ford in the river where the great copper bowl hung from a tree with all the shields belonging to the imprisoned knights. Riding towards him was a huge knight on a great war horse and driving another horse before him. Trussed up and slung over its back lay Sir Gaheris.

"Hold!" Sir Lancelot called out. "You have one of the Knights of the Round Table there as prisoner. I must challenge you, for it is my duty to release him."

"If you are one of the Knights of the Round Table I shall gladly fight you," called out the knight, "for my purpose is to defeat all the followers of King Arthur."

A tremendous contest between the two knights followed. First it looked as though the huge knight would win, then Sir Lancelot seemed to have the upper hand. Backwards and forwards they went, while Gaheris, powerless to help, watched from his uncomfortable position lying across his horse's saddle. Eventually the two men paused for breath. "You fight well," the large man said. "I am tempted to call a truce, for you have given me a better fight than anyone else. I'll allow you to ride away from here alive, provided you are not the one man I most wish to kill."

"Tell me your name and that of the man you most wish to kill?" asked Sir Lancelot.

"My name is Sir Turquin, and the one man I will never let go alive is Sir Lancelot of the Lake, for he slew my brother Sir Carados."

"Then we fight to the death," Sir Lancelot declared. "I slew your brother Carados. He was an evil man with many evil deeds to his name. I am none other than Sir Lancelot of the Lake."

At once the two were fighting again. Gradually Sir Lancelot forced Sir Turquin back, and then dealt him a great blow. When he saw his opponent must die, he went to Sir Gaheris and untied him.

"Take this scoundrel's keys," he said, "and release any prisoners in his house, while I wash my wounds in the river."

Sir Gaheris found many friends imprisoned in the house. Not only Sir Lionel and Sir Hector, but Sir Kay and others from Camelot. They made much of him, but Sir Gaheris said, "It is not me you should be thanking, but Sir Lancelot. He is the best fighter in all the world and it is he who has at last killed this cruel Sir Turquin. You can thank him when he has finished cleaning his wounds."

But Sir Lancelot, on finding he was not badly hurt, rode on before his friends could come out, for he still did not feel ready to return to Camelot.

* * *

Some days later Sir Lancelot came across a maiden, distraught with grief. "Will you help me?" she asked. "My brother Sir Meliot lies badly wounded after a fight and will die if I cannot get the sword and part of the burial robe of a knight who lies dead in the Chapel Perilous. Will you ride and bring these things to my brother. But beware, the chapel is guarded by an evil enchantress called Allewes, and she will ensnare you if she can."

"I will go gladly," said Sir Lancelot, "for Sir Meliot and I are both Knights of the Round Table."

As Sir Lancelot approached the Chapel Perilous, thirty knights in black armour, with their helmets pulled far over their faces, challenged him. Afraid, but not showing it, Sir Lancelot drew his sword and held up his shield and advanced boldly through them. They drew back and he entered the chapel. There in the dim light he saw a corpse stretched out and waiting for burial. By his right hand lay a sword. Sir Lancelot cut off a piece of his burial robe. As he picked up the sword the earth shook, but Lancelot did not waver and walked out of the chapel. The knights in black threatened again, but as before, when he showed no fear, they stood back.

76

Now he was challenged by a strange damsel who said, "Leave that sword here, or you will die!"

"I will not leave the sword," replied Sir Lancelot.

"You speak wisely," she said. "If you had given it up, you never would have reached King Arthur's court again. But now you must kiss me, before you pass."

"If I were to kiss you, it would be a sinful kiss," replied Sir Lancelot.

The lady started to weep, saying, "Alas, you have failed to fall into the trap I have laid for you. I am Allewes the Sorceress, and I have loved you for many years." Lancelot made the sign of the cross, and when he looked again the damsel was no longer there.

Now Sir Lancelot rode with haste to join Sir Meliot's sister, and together they went to where Sir Meliot lay weak from loss of blood. Lancelot touched him with the sword and bound his wound with the strip of cloth, and Sir Meliot began to gain strength. Happy to have been of service to a fellow Knight of the Round Table, Sir Lancelot rode on.

* * *

Lancelot continued his adventures, always putting evil aside and winning glory through his bravery. After nearly a year of wandering he was returning to Camelot for the High Feast at Whitsun, when he came across Sir Kay who was being attacked by robbers. He rescued Sir Kay, and early the next morning while Sir Kay was still asleep, he rode off wearing Sir Kay's armour, and riding Sir Kay's horse. Sir Kay was not popular, and many of the knights took pleasure in teasing him and knocking him off his horse, and Sir Lancelot thought he might have some good sport disguised as Sir Kay.

Before long he met up with four Knights of the Round Table, his brother Sir Hector, Sir Segramore, Sir Uwain and Sir Gawain. They too were riding towards Camelot for the Whitsun High Feast. At once, Sir Segramore challenged Sir Lancelot, thinking him to be Sir Kay, and sure that he would fall to the ground quickly. But Sir Lancelot was too swift for him, and to Sir Segramore's astonishment it was he who was very soon flat on his back on the ground. Sir

Uwain and Sir Hector fared no better. Gawain looked carefully at this man they all thought to be Sir Kay. "I believe he might be Lancelot even though he is wearing Kay's armour and riding Kay's horse," he thought to himself, for he had noticed a certain trick he used with his lance, which he had seen Sir Lancelot use the previous year at Camelot. Even Sir Gawain found himself unseated in a matter of seconds.

Now Sir Lancelot raised his helmet so they could see who he was. There was a shout of laughter and they rode on together in great good humour to Camelot. Sir Kay followed behind with Sir Lancelot's horse and armour, and even he, lacking in a sense of humour as he was, had to admit that Sir Lancelot was a brave knight and worthy of the Round Table.

King Arthur delighted in all the stories he heard, and congratulated Sir Lancelot. The tale of how he had defeated the wicked Sir Turquin and sent Gaheris in to release the prisoners in Turquin's house was already a popular tale in court. Sir Meliot recounted how Sir Lancelot had confounded the sorceress Allewes and saved his life, and Sir Kay added his praises for Sir Lancelot's help to him.

"You are the finest knight at the Round Table," said Arthur, with pride.

Only when he looked into Queen Guinevere's eyes did Sir Lancelot feel ashamed, for he knew he could never be truly worthy of all that was best at King Arthur's court when he loved the king's wife.

10

SIR GAWAIN AND THE GREEN KNIGHT

A great fire roared in the hearth as the Knights of the Round Table gathered at Camelot for a New Year's Feast. At King Arthur's court, no feast could start until some adventure or quest had been undertaken. So the knights sat and waited for what might come. Which of them would ride out to perform some feat from which he might never return? The young men all hoped that their turn might arrive when they would prove their strength and valour, but their hopes were mixed with fear.

There was a stir by the door, and silence fell over the gathered company as a huge knight, unknown to them all, rode in through the great doors at the end of the hall. None had ever seen a stranger man for he was green from head to toe. His hair, his skin, his clothes were all green, and he carried a great axe with a sharp blade that glinted green and gold. Each man sized up his own strength against the newcomer and shrank from the thought of combat with him.

"Who is the leader of this band of youths?" the Green Knight called out in a deep and powerful voice. "I thought I was coming to the court of King Arthur where all the bravest warriors would be found, but I see only pale weaklings before me."

"I am King Arthur," the king spoke out, "and all these men you see are brave fighters. Do you seek combat?"

"I came with a challenge, but I can see I shall leave disappointed for I don't like to fight with beardless boys and chicken-hearted knights," roared the green knight.

"Tell us your challenge," said King Arthur, "and we shall meet it."

The visiting knight sat on his horse and looked around the hall, his green eyes travelled from man to man, and he smiled a grim smile as he turned back to King Arthur. "I challenge one of you to strike a blow on my body with this axe of mine. If I survive, the knight who strikes the blow must meet me in exactly one year and one day's time and receive a similar blow. And I shall be the one to choose where the blow will fall!"

No one moved, no one spoke, until King Arthur stepped forward. "I accept your challenge, stranger! I will strike the blow with your axe where you direct. You will see we are no band of cowards!"

At once, voices were raised in protest. Surely no man would come out alive from fighting a knight such as this and King Arthur, their leader and high king, should not risk his life in this way.

Then Sir Gawain stepped out before them all. "Uncle, allow me to be the one to strike the Green Knight as he asks. I would like another chance to prove that I am a worthy knight."

Arthur knew Gawain still carried the shame of killing a lady on his first quest, and saw how the young man wanted to take on this challenge, and so he nodded. "Ay, nephew, you can show this stranger that the Knights of the Round Table stand for courage, strength and honour."

Slowly the Green Knight dismounted and knelt before Sir Gawain. "Take my axe," he instructed "and strike me here" and he pointed to the back of his neck. Then kneeling down he placed his head on the floor, bared his neck, and waited for the blow.

Gawain hesitated. Such a blow would kill the Green Knight who knelt there unarmed. What was he to do? "I suspected you would not have the courage," the green knight said in a stern voice as he knelt there. Gawain hesitated no longer. He raised the axe and swung it so that it fell swift and sure on the back of the Green Knight's neck. A gasp went up as the knight's head separated from his body.

The world swam before Gawain. Then a louder gasp echoed around the hall as the headless knight rose to his feet, and walked across the floor. Now, holding his head under one arm, he remounted his horse and held out his hand for his axe.

The disembodied voice then spoke, addressing Sir Gawain. "I will see you in a year and a day, at the Green Chapel, where you must face my blow." And the headless knight rode out of the great hall of Camelot.

As the year passed, Gawain's thoughts often strayed to the meeting he was to have with the Green Knight on New Year's Day. Life seemed even more sweet and precious with the possibility he might never see the spring flowers again or hear the birds sing in another summer. As the autumn leaves were falling on the forest floor and the days grew shorter, he prepared for the journey to the Green Chapel, wherever that might be.

"You will find the Green Chapel," Arthur advised, "but part of the quest must be looking for it. The Green Knight rode out of the northwest, so ride that way and ask as you go."

So Gawain rode out on his horse called Gringolot, scarcely daring to look behind at Camelot as he departed, so sure he was that he would never see it again. He rode through forest and over heathland, he crossed rivers and passed through villages, asking wherever he went where he might find the Green Chapel. Some shook their heads, while others said, "Keep going in that direction," pointing to the north or to the west.

By Christmas Eve Gawain was far from Camelot, and in despair that he would not find the Green Chapel in time to keep his promised meeting with the Green Knight on New Year's Day. Both he and his horse were weary and mud-spattered as they travelled through a dark and lonely stretch of forest. As daylight began to fade he saw the towers of a fine castle, and rode towards it. "Perhaps they will give me and my horse shelter for the night and tell me how far I have to go," he told himself as he rode up to the castle gates.

"My master, Sir Bertilak, and his lady will welcome you at this Christmas season," the guard said, as he called for a groom to take Gawain's horse Gringolot to the stables and summoned a servant to lead Gawain to the great hall.

"Come in, and welcome! Tell us who you are and what we can do for you," a loud voice bellowed across the hall. Gawain found himself being greeted by a large man with a cheerful smiling face. Beside him stood his attractive wife.

"My name is Sir Gawain, and I am from King Arthur's court at Camelot," Gawain told them. I seek shelter for my horse and myself for the night, and I am also looking for directions to the Green Chapel where I have to fulfil a promise on New Year's Day."

"You can stay here and keep my lady and myself company until New Year's Day, for the Green Chapel is no more than two hours' ride from here. Any knight from King Arthur's court is most welcome for we have heard glowing tales of the company he has gathered at Camelot."

For four days Gawain feasted and drank with Sir Bertilak and his wife, and while he tried to enjoy himself, Gawain only thought of the meeting with the Green Knight at the Green Chapel, and how this might be his last Christmas. Then his host said, "For the next three days I shall be out hunting. At this time of the year I always hunt for wild geese and for deer and wild boar in the forests around here. You would probably prefer to spend the days here preparing for your meeting at the Green Chapel. I'd like to suggest we make a bargain."

"You are right. I'd like to stay here quietly for three more days," Gawain agreed. "So what do you propose?"

"Each day when I return from the hunt I shall present you with any prize I have gained. You in return shall give me any prize you gain here."

Gawain could seen no harm in this suggestion, and so he agreed to it. He thought in fact, that he stood to gain more than Sir Bertilak, for what prize could he get in the castle?

It was late in the morning when Sir Gawain awoke the next day. He opened his eyes to find Sir Bertilak's beautiful wife leaning over his bed. "Ah, you are awake at last," she said in her soft and lovely voice. "While my lord is out hunting you can amuse me with tales of the brave deeds and gallant knights at Camelot."

Some pleasant hours passed, which Gawain enjoyed, for the lady flattered and teased him until he felt he would do anything she asked, or almost anything. For when she asked him to hold her in his arms, he turned away, remembering he had come on this quest to prove to the Knights of the Round Table that he was a man of honour.

"That I cannot do, for your husband is a generous host, and I cannot behave with dishonour."

"What a goody-goody you are," she pouted. "Would one little kiss be too much for your honour?"

Gawain laughed and gave her a small kiss, and then sent her from his room.

At dusk, Sir Bertilak rode in with his hunting party. From his saddle were tied two wild geese, both shot through the heart by arrows. Gawain met them in the courtyard and Sir Bertilak handed the geese to Gawain, saying, "Here is my part of the bargain!"

As Sir Bertilak dismounted, Gawain placed his hands on his host's shoulders, and kissed him lightly on the cheek. "And that is my part of the bargain," he said, "for I gained one kiss today in this castle."

A hearty guffaw was the reply. "I see you are a man of honour, Sir Gawain. I like you even more now than I did before! Come let us go and join my wife in the hall."

Sir Bertilak rode out early the next day, and Gawain once more awoke to find Sir Bertilak's wife by his bed. She flirted and laughed with him for most of the day, and again begged him to take her in his arms, for she found him so attractive. Gawain firmly refused, but this time before she left, they exchanged two kisses. He was disturbed, for he found her so lovely. "I must leave the castle today," he told himself, "or I will bring shame on King Arthur's court if I allow myself to love this lady. But it would be rude to ride away when my host is out hunting. I shall depart early tomorrow."

When he heard the hunting party return, he strode into the courtyard determined to tell Sir Bertilak that he must leave early the next morning. But Sir Bertilak presented him with a fine stag that lay across the back of one of the huntsmen's horses and clapped Sir Gawain warmly on the back when he kissed his host twice. "Only two kisses! What an honourable fellow you are!" And he would not hear of Sir Gawain's departure. "I can assure you, the Green Chapel is two hours' ride from here. You would find nowhere else to spend the night before the ordeal which is obviously causing you concern. I shall send a servant with you to show you the way the day after tomorrow. Come now, let us go and dine with my lady. And no more talk of leaving us a day early. You would disappoint us both, and make us feel we had not looked after you well."

As Gawain feared, the next morning Sir Bertilak's wife was once more in his room when he awoke. They laughed and flirted for some time and then she begged Gawain to love her. He shook his head, and held her at arms' length.

"If we cannot be lovers, you must at least take this silken girdle I have, and wear it tomorrow in the contest you are to have at the Green Chapel, for it will ensure your safety," and she slipped off the green belt she wore at her waist. Gawain held it close to him and longed to keep it as a memento of his visit. "Wear it next to your skin," she urged, "and do not let my husband see it or he will be furious with jealousy. He might even kill you before you leave for the Green Chapel tomorrow."

Gawain thought of the next day, and how he feared for his life. With this magic girdle next to his skin he might yet ride back safely to Camelot. He slipped the girdle into his shirt, and they kissed three times.

That evening Sir Bertilak presented him with a fine wild boar that they had hunted and killed, and Sir Gawain gave his host three kisses as they greeted each other in the courtyard.

"Three kisses today, and no more?" he queried.

Gawain replied, "Three kisses was my gain today," and said no word of the silken girdle.

A shadow hung over Gawain as they ate and drank that evening for he feared it would be his last meal, his last evening alive.

At first light, he mounted Gringolot and rode out from Sir Bertilak's castle with a servant riding beside him to show him the way. At length they came to the head of a valley, and there the servant stopped. "If you follow the river you will come to the Green Chapel where the valley broadens out and you can cross the river. It is a magical place. Not many pass that way. I wish you well, Sir Gawain," and he rode back the way they had come.

Sir Gawain followed his instructions, and as he approached the ford he saw a mound like an ancient burial ground covered in turf, and coming from within he heard the sound of steel on steel. Could this be the Green Chapel?

"I have an appointment to meet the Green Knight!" he called out. "Have I come to the right place?"

A great loud voice called back, "You are at the Green Chapel, Sir Gawain. Wait there while I finish sharpening my axe for the blow that is coming your way." A shiver ran down Sir Gawain's spine, and his hand strayed to his shirt where the lady's silken girdle lay against his skin.

Gringolot suddenly jumped, as out from the turf-covered mound strode the Green Knight, as huge and horrible as he had been the year before. "Kneel before me, Sir Gawain, and prepare to lose your head," he roared.

Sir Gawain left his horse loose, fearing he would not be alive to untie him if he were tethered to a tree, and knelt on the ground before the Green Knight. He heard the air whistle as the gleaming axe was swung, and in that split second Gawain's nerve failed, and he pulled himself to one side. The axe thudded into the ground, its sharp blade biting deep into the earth.

"What? Are you a coward, and you a knight from King Arthur's court?" the Green Knight roared. "A bargain is a bargain, you know!"

Gawain knelt before the Green Knight once more. Again he heard the air whistle as the axe swung, but this time he did not flinch. To his amazement the axe missed him by a hair's breadth, and buried itself again in the earth.

"One more try!" the Green Knight roared and Gawain quaked inwardly as he heard the axe approach, but he did not move a muscle. This time the axe touched his neck, grazing it, then slipped off, landing on the grass.

"Enough!" cried Gawain, springing to his feet. "I have received your blow and I am not dead. We will fight each other now with our swords!" and he pulled his sword from its scabbard. As he turned to face his opponent his sword fell from his hand, for there before him stood not the Green Knight, but Sir Bertilak, his cheerful host of the past eight days.

"Yes, Gawain, I am both Sir Bertilak and the Green Knight. I can

change from one to the other through the magic of this place. The first two blows which missed you were for the days when you gave me an honest response to the prizes you gained in my castle, while I was out hunting. But the third blow, where I grazed your neck was deliberate for you were not honest with me the third day. You carry my lady's silken girdle next to your heart in the belief that it might save your life. You are young and right to value your life, and so I forgive you this small dishonesty. Had you fallen to the temptations my lady put before you, I would have killed you today. But you have proved a worthy Knight of the Round Table for you put honour above your own desires."

"I still find it hard to comprehend," said Sir Gawain.

"There are many things to do with magic that we do not need to understand, Sir Gawain," replied Sir Bertilak. "What I know is that King Arthur is fortunate to have a knight like you at his court. Ride now to Camelot and tell them of your adventure."

When Sir Gawain rode in through the gates of Camelot there were many who had not expected to see him again. They gathered round and heard his story, and when he drew out the silken girdle and told them of his shame in concealing it, they praised him for his courage. Before long it became the fashion for the bravest knights to wear a belt of green in honour of Sir Gawain.

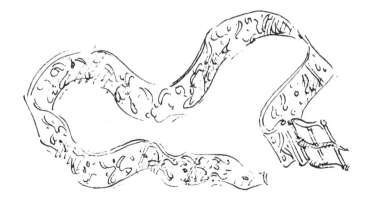

11

THE KNIGHT OF THE KITCHEN

It was Whitsun, and many of King Arthur's court had come to Camelot for their traditional feast. Some travellers were seen approaching on foot and a strange sight they made, for one was a young man who stood taller than any man at Camelot, while following behind came a dwarf. They walked confidently into the hall and stopped before King Arthur.

"My lord," said the tall, lanky youth, "I have come to ask three things of you."

"Ask what you will," said King Arthur. He thought the young man looked like a good swordsman and horseman and could be a welcome addition to the Knights of the Round Table.

"I ask that you allow me to stay here in Camelot for a year, and that you provide me with food and clothing."

"That you can have most definitely," King Arthur replied. "I'd grant the same to any man who asked me. You look as though you will be a brave knight. Tell me, who are you? And what are your two other requests?"

"I do not wish to tell you my name for the moment. And I should like to ask for the two other favours in one year's time," said the tall young man.

"As you like," replied King Arthur, and he called over Sir Kay, who was the steward in his household. "Take our young visitor, who prefers not to give his name, and see that he is fed and clothed. Let him have only the very best. He will be part of our household for the next twelve months."

Sir Kay, who was often bad-tempered and mean, grumbled

at what he was asked to do. "The newcomer cannot be from a noble family, or he would have asked for a horse and armour. He does not deserve the best. He must work for his keep in the kitchen if he wishes to stay here."

In the kitchen the young man was teased, for he did not know how to turn the spit or bake the bread. His hands were white and soft-skinned for he was not accustomed to any manual work, and so they nicknamed him Beaumains which means Pretty Hands. Soon he was known to all as Beaumains. He was popular, for he worked hard and was good-tempered. If ever he got the chance to come out and watch the knights on the jousting-field, he would be there. Sir Lancelot and Sir Gawain were both kind to him, if they saw him, for like King Arthur, they thought he had the makings of a fine knight.

The following year, at the Whitsun feast, a young lady rode up to the hall and spoke to King Arthur. "My sister, the Lady of Lyonesse, is in dire need of help. All her lands have been taken and she has been imprisoned by the Red Knight of the Red Lands. Will you send someone to come to her aid?"

At this, Beaumains, who had come into the hall, stepped forward. "My lord king, it is time now for me to ask my two further favours. Please allow me to go on this quest and rescue the Lady of Lyonnesse from the Red Knight of the Red Lands."

"The quest shall by yours," said King Arthur. "And your other favour?

"That Sir Lancelot rides with me for part of the way, and makes me a knight when he decides I deserve it. I should like above all to be knighted by the brave and good Sir Lancelot of the Lake."

The king glanced at Lancelot, who nodded, and so King Arthur told Beaumains that both his requests were granted.

At this, there was a scream of rage from the lady seeking help for her sister. "What, you will send me a kitchen hand when the finest knights in the kingdom are here? You think very little of my sister's plight if this is all you can do for her! I'd rather no help at all than help from this kitchen lout!" So saying, she turned and angrily rode away.

In the courtyard, where many went to see her depart, they found the dwarf who had arrived with Beaumains a year ago. He was holding the bridle of a large horse and a sword. Beaumains mounted the horse, and carrying neither shield nor spear, but only the sword, rode after the lady as quickly as he could. Sir Kay, who was furious that King Arthur had shown favour to his kitchen boy, rode out after him. He was determined to show Beaumains how cross he was. Following hard behind Sir Kay rode Sir Lancelot.

As Beaumains caught up with the lady, Sir Kay called out, "Stop, you kitchen boy." And when Beaumains ignored him, he called out again, "Stop! Do you not know who I am?"

Beaumains turned and looked at him and said, "Yes, I know you for a most ungallant and unfriendly knight, and for this you should beware of me."

Immediately Sir Kay raised his spear and charged straight at him. Beaumains, who was armed only with a sword, used it with lightning speed as Sir Kay came level, and with the point caught Sir Kay in a crack of his armour. Sir Kay fell to the ground and lay there as though he were dead. Beaumains took Sir Kay's shield and spear, and began to ride on when Sir Lancelot, who had been watching, challenged him.

They fought for a while, first on horseback and then on foot, each attacking the other fiercely and defending himself with skill. Backwards and forwards they went, like two wild boars in battle, until Sir Lancelot, who was amazed at the young man's fighting skills, called a halt.

"We have no great quarrel. Let us not fight to the bitter end."

"You are right, but it does me good to fight an opponent as strong as you," Beaumains replied.

"And I wondered at times if I could hold my own against you," Sir Lancelot told him.

"Do you judge me fit to be a knight?" asked Beaumains.

"I do. You have proved yourself worthy. But I can't make you a knight until I know your name."

"I am Gareth, youngest son of King Lot of the Orkneys and Queen Morgause," replied the tall young man.

"Then you are King Arthur's nephew. He will be glad to hear this, for he liked you from the start. But how is it that your brothers, Sir

Gawain, Sir Agravaine and Sir Gaheris, who are all at Camelot, did not recognise you?"

"They left home eight or ten years ago, when I was only a small boy. I have grown into a man while they were gone."

Gareth knelt before Sir Lancelot, who touched him on either shoulder with his sword, and said, "Arise Sir Gareth. Go on now with your quest and rescue the lady from the Red Knight of the Red Lands if you can."

Sir Lancelot turned back the way he had come, and seeing Sir Kay still lying on the ground, arranged for him to be carried back to Camelot.

Now Beaumains caught up with the lady who had ridden on while he was fighting with Sir Lancelot. As he drew level with her he said, "Tell me your name, for we have far to ride together."

"My name is Linnet, but I don't know why I should tell you, you kitchen lout. You stink of cooking! Return where you belong and leave me to find another champion for my sister."

"I cannot return until I have saved your sister, for I have undertaken a quest, and I must go on until I achieve it," he told her in a firm voice.

As they argued, a man came running through the wood, "Help! Help!" he called. "My master has been captured by six thieves."

"Show us where he is," cried Beaumains, "and I shall rescue him!"

"But six against one! It's impossible!" the man protested. He led them to a clearing where they found a knight tied up and surrounded by six violent men. Beaumains attacked three at once and slew them all, and then caught up with the other three who were running off, and killed them.

"You have saved my life. How may I thank you?" the knight asked.

"Today I was knighted by Sir Lancelot. That is reward enough for me."

"If I can do nothing else, I trust you will both come and eat and sleep in my castle which is nearby," said the knight.

So Beaumains, or Sir Gareth to give him his true name, and Linnet rode to the knight's castle. There she continued to rail and scold Sir Gareth, refusing even to sit at the same table as him, until the knight took her to task. "He is a brave and gallant knight. Shame on you for treating him so." And he moved to sit at a side table with Sir Gareth.

When they rode out the next day, Linnet was still abusing Sir Gareth, who replied politely to whatever she said. As they approached a river they saw two knights who challenged them. Sir Gareth rode into the water and fought both of them at the same time. He knocked one off his horse into the river and the other on to the river bank. Still Linnet scolded him in a shrill voice, this time for taking unfair advantage of the knights when their horses had slipped.

In the afternoon they came to a land that was blackened as though it had been burnt. Waiting for them was a knight dressed all in black, with a black shield and a black spear. He sat on a huge black horse.

"So, Lady Linnet, is this all the help that King Arthur was able to provide? I will knock down this lad in an instant and then you will no longer be bothered by him."

With no further warning, he raised his spear and charged, expecting to throw the young man from his horse at the first blow. But Sir Gareth faced his charge and fought bravely. Before long the Black Knight lay on the ground, dead.

"I shall take his armour, for I see I have need of it," said Sir Gareth.

As soon as he had dressed himself in the Black Knight's armour, he rode on to catch up with the Lady Linnet, who scolded him afresh.

"You can be as rude and unfriendly as you like," Sir Gareth told her, but I shall ride with you until my quest is completed."

Ahead they saw a knight dressed all in green. "Greetings!" he called out to Linnet. "Do you ride with my brother, the Black Knight?"

"I ride with a knave from King Arthur's kitchens who slew your brother by treachery, and now wears his armour."

"I fought your brother in fair combat," said Sir Gareth, "and I will fight you too, if you insist."

The knight in green blew on a horn, and two ladies came from a green pavilion with his shield and his spear. With no more ceremony, the knight in green charged at Sir Gareth. They fought hard for a while, first on horseback and then on foot, until gradually it looked as though Sir Gareth must win. "Shame on you," called out Linnet to the knight in green. "Will you be beaten by a kitchen boy!"

The knight in green was spurred on by this and dealt Sir Gareth a mighty blow. Now rage swept through Sir Gareth, and he made a tremendous effort and forced his opponent down, until he lay at Sir Gareth's feet.

"Mercy! Mercy!" he cried.

"I'll only grant you mercy if the lady asks for it."

"And I shall ask nothing from you, kitchen boy!"

"Then I must kill this knight," said Gareth, raising his sword.

"No, stop, you kitchen knave. Spare this man's life," Linnet called out.

So Gareth stopped his sword in mid air, and said to the knight in green, "Ride to King Arthur's court with thirty men, and say you were sent by the Knight of the Kitchen."

"Tomorrow I will go to Camelot as you say. Tonight I hope you will be guests in my castle."

Throughout the evening Linnet continued to be rude to Sir Gareth, until the knight in green took her aside. "This is no kitchen boy. He is a fine young man from a noble family. We may not know his name, but you do him wrong to treat him so."

The next day Linnet rode on with Sir Gareth, while the knight in green gathered together thirty men and departed for Camelot. After riding in silence for some time, Linnet said, "You need ride no more with me. As I said before, I will find another champion."

"I will ride with you until I save your sister, or until I die in the attempt," Sir Gareth replied.

"Then we will soon be parted, for we approach the lands of the Blue Knight, and he will surely kill you!"

It seemed to Sir Gareth she spoke a little less harshly than on previous occasions, and he thought she looked on him in a more kindly way, too.

They now approached a field where there was a blue pavilion and a knight in blue armour with a blue banner. He challenged Sir Gareth, and they fought. When Sir Gareth proved himself the victor,

Linnet spoke up, but more gently than she had before, asking for mercy for the Blue Knight, and Sir Gareth spared him, saying, "Ride to King Arthur's court with forty knights and say you were sent by the Knight of the Kitchen."

"I will ride tomorrow, but tonight you shall stay in my castle."

That evening Linnet told the Blue Knight how they were riding to rescue her sister, the Lady Lyonesse, from the Red Knight of the Red Lands.

"Ah, the Red Knight of the Red Lands. He is the fiercest knight you can imagine," he said. "Can I suggest that I confer knighthood on your young companion? He fights well enough to defeat anyone – except possibly the Red Knight of the Red Lands. But to challenge him he should be a knight himself."

"Thank you," replied Sir Gareth, "but since I left King Arthur's court, Sir Lancelot of the Lake has already made me a knight."

"There is no one better from whom to receive your knighthood. Will you tell us who you are?"

"My name is Gareth, and I am the youngest son of King Lot of the Orkneys and Queen Morgause."

Now Linnet looked at him with astonishment. "I have treated you very badly," she said, with surprising humility.

"You have spoken to me very harshly, but because of my anger at the way you treated me I think I was driven to find greater courage and skill when fighting. Your words did me no harm and they may have done me good."

Linnet and Sir Gareth rode on towards the west and in time they came to a wood. From the branches of all the trees hung dead knights. "We are approaching the castle where my sister is imprisoned. These dead men are all the knights who have already tried to rescue her. I fear your body will soon be hanging from a tree like theirs," she whispered.

It was a grim sight, and Gareth shuddered to see so many dead men who had not been given a decent burial. Beyond the wood was a castle, and before the castle was a red pavilion. Gareth took up a great horn that hung from the branches of one of the trees and started to blow it.

"Stop!" cried Linnet. "I am told the Red Knight grows stronger every hour before noon, and weaker each hour as evening approaches. Do not summon him until the evening."

"Lady, I cannot fight a man when he is at his weakest. I must fight him when he is at full strength." And Gareth blew a tremendous blast on the horn.

From the pavilion rode out a huge knight, dressed in red, with a red shield and a red banner. As Gareth looked up at the castle he saw in a window the face of a beautiful woman. He only had time for a glimpse, before the Red Knight of the Red Lands was thundering towards him with his spear raised.

The fight between Sir Gareth and the Knight of the Red Lands was fierce and desperate. At last it seemed that both had lost so much blood that neither would live. Then the Red Knight cried out for mercy and Gareth paused. "Tell me why you keep the Lady Lyonesse imprisoned."

"I loved a lady who swore vengeance on Sir Lancelot. I promised to kill all those who had anything to do with King Arthur's court. I was bewitched by her. Morgan le Fay was her name. It was she who told me to take the lands of the Lady Lyonesse and keep her imprisoned."

"I shall leave it to the Lady Lyonesse to decide if your life be spared. If she says you shall live, you must go to King Arthur's court and beg forgiveness from Sir Gawain and Sir Lancelot and all those you have harmed."

Linnet went to her sister in the castle and told her how Sir Gareth had come from King Arthur's court to rescue her from the Red Knight of the Red Lands. "He has now defeated the Red Knight of the Red Lands in single combat, and says it is up to you to grant him mercy or not."

The Lady Lyonesse granted the mercy he requested, and so the Red Knight rode to Camelot. "I have been sent by a young man who defeated me in combat. He sends me to beg forgiveness for capturing the Lady Lyonesse."

"It sounds as though our Knight of the Kitchen has fulfilled his quest," said King Arthur. "Is it not time we heard his name?"

When Sir Lancelot told them the young man was Gareth, younger brother of Sir Gawain, they were all overjoyed.

Sir Gareth stayed at the castle where the Lady Lyonesse had been imprisoned, while he recovered from his wounds. He stayed too because he loved her. At first she was quite cold towards him, but after some time she found she loved him and agreed to marry him.

The story of how the Knight of the Kitchen fought the Black Knight, the Green Knight, the Blue Knight, and the Red Knight of the Red Lands, to rescue the Lady Lyonesse who became his bride, was a favourite among King Arthur's friends and the Knights of the Round Table. Only Sir Kay would frown and disappear when the story was told and retold.

12

TRISTAN AND FAIR ISEULT

While King Arthur had his court at Camelot, the ruler of Cornwall was King Mark. His nephew Tristan was famed in stories told by travelling harpists, and the Knights of the Round Table, like many others, loved to hear of Tristan's courage, and of the strange events in his life. "I hope he will come to Camelot. Merlin hinted that a place awaits him at the Round Table," Arthur said to Guinevere on more than one occasion.

One day, a tall, good-looking harpist arrived at Camelot and was made welcome. "I come from Cornwall," he told the king and queen as he talked to them in the great hall.

"Then you may have met Tristan, whose fame has spread far," Queen Guinevere said. "Can you tell us some stories about him?"

"Yes, I can sing some songs and tell some tales about Tristan, but his life is full of sadness," replied the harpist. "I shall bring little cheer to your court."

"Tell us all the same," replied King Arthur, "for we hope one day to welcome Tristan here."

So they settled down for an evening's story-telling. King Arthur and Queen Guinevere were present, and many others besides. The harpist sat with quiet dignity, and plucked his harp strings rather as Merlin used to, and started on his tale.

There was trouble for Tristan, even before his birth, the harpist told them. His parents were attacked by a fierce neighbour called Rivalin and his father was killed in the fighting. His mother, who was sister to King Mark of Cornwall, fled to the forests to hide from Rivalin and his soldiers and there her baby son was born. She was weak and knew she had not long to live, so she called over Rual, a faithful follower, and entrusted her baby to him.

"Call him Tristan," she said, "for he is born of sorrow. Teach him all you can, and when he is a grown man, take him to my brother's court in Cornwall." She died shortly after speaking these words and Rual took the tiny baby to his home.

Rual and his wife tended the boy and loved him as their own, and taught him many things, and Gorvenal, the wise man taught him more besides. In this way Tristan learnt swordsmanship, and how to ride and joust, and how to play chess and play the harp.

One day, a trading vessel from the far north stopped in the harbour near Rual's home, and the captain invited Tristan on board. While he and Tristan ate a meal the ship sailed and Tristan found he was a captive and was being taken to another country across the sea. But then a violent storm blew up and the ship was nearly wrecked. Many of the sailors said their prisoner had brought bad luck to the ship, and insisted that when the wind abated, he was put ashore. So as the seas grew calmer, a small boat put out and dropped Tristan on a beach in a place he did not know.

Tristan had landed in Cornwall, and he soon made his way to King Mark's court, although he did not know he was the king's nephew. There he was accepted as a fine swordsman, and became popular at the court.

Rual, meanwhile, had sent out a search far and wide for the missing youth, and word came to him eventually that he was at King Mark's court in Cornwall. "So fate works," said Rual, "for Tristan has gone where I was supposed to take him." Rual now came to Cornwall to tell Tristan who he was.

Some years earlier, the people of Cornwall had been defeated in battle by King Gurman from Ireland, and King Mark had agreed to send thirty youths from Cornwall whenever they were demanded to serve the Irish King. Now King Gurman sent a kinsman called Marhout, who was a great strong warrior, demanding once again that thirty young men should return to Ireland. Sorrow fell across the whole court for many families would lose a beloved son.

"Uncle, shame on you!" cried Tristan. "Too many years have gone by for you to continue to send our best young men to King Gurman when they are demanded.''

''The only alternative is for someone to fight Marhout in single combat, and if our man should lose, we would have to send another. And lose he would, for Marhout is the strongest man you have ever seen,'' King Mark told Tristan with a sad shake of his head.

Tristan insisted, however, that he himself should fight Marhout, and the challenge was made. Marhout agreed, and a small island, where no one lived and where there would be no witnesses, was chosen for the fight. Marhout came first, and when Tristan landed he cast his boat off from the shore. ''You are a fool, young man, to let your boat go!'' roared Marhout.

''Not so, for only one of us will leave this island alive, and your boat awaits that man,'' called back Tristan, and he drew his sword.

It was a fierce and bitter fight, and there were times when Tristan felt his strength failing, so strong and vigorous was his opponent. But he fought on, determined not to give in. Marhout, too, was finding it hard to get past the young man's guard, but at last his sword thrust past Tristan's shield and into his thigh. ''Ah,'' roared out the great Irish giant, ''now you will surely die for my sword was dipped in poison before I left Ireland.''

''I show no mercy to those who fight by unfair means,'' cried Tristan, and he swung his sword in a great arc and brought it crashing down on Marhout's head. As Tristan pulled his sword free a fragment of the blade remained embedded in the bone. Marhout sank to his knees and cried out that he was defeated. Weak and exhausted by the fight, Tristan climbed into the boat and rowed slowly back to the shore where he was greeted with joy by his uncle, King Mark. The Irish ship which should have taken the thirty Cornish youths to King Gurman, picked up Marhout, wounded and dying, and bore him back to Ireland.

King Gurman's daughter, known to all as the fair Iseult, knew more of medicine and healing than any other in Ireland at that time. She tended Marhout on his return, but for all her skills she could not save his life. After his death she removed from his skull the fragment of Tristan's sword, and kept it in a small box, saying, ''Whoever struck that blow was a brave man.''

Meanwhile Tristan's wound from the poisoned sword did not heal and he gradually became weaker and weaker. ''I must go to Ireland. Whoever put the poison on the sword's blade will know the cure,'' he said.

''But King Gurman has sworn death to Marhout's killer. You will die if you go there,'' King Mark told him.

''And I will die if I stay here, so I prefer to go and take a chance with my life in Ireland,'' declared the young man. Disguising himself as a harpist, he set out for Ireland.

When he reached King Gurman's court, he sang so beautifully that he was invited to stay for a while, and the king arranged for Iseult to learn the harp from the visitor. ''See if you can help his wound to heal, too,'' the king advised his daughter. ''He tells me he received it when the ship he came on was attacked.''

So for many months Tristan stayed at the court of King Gurman. Iseult tended his wounded thigh, using her knowledge of herbs and all the skills she had learnt from her mother. While his wound healed, Iseult learnt to sing and play the harp, and as the weeks and months went by they fell deeply in love. ''I cannot ask for her as my wife, for I will be killed as soon as my true identity is known,'' Tristan told himself. Not knowing how else to control his passion, he slipped away one night and returned to Cornwall.

* * *

King Mark was not married. He knew he should find a wife, but none of the ladies he had considered seemed right for him. Then, one day, when sitting on a balcony in his castle in Cornwall a swallow alighted. Round its neck was a long auburn hair. King Mark took it from the bird and held it up. ''If I could find the lady whose head this hair comes from and marry her, then I would find happiness, for I am sure she has great beauty,'' he said.

Tristan recognised the hair at once as being from the fair Iseult, and told the king he knew the lady from whose head it came. ''Will you go to Ireland as my envoy and ask for her hand in marriage?'' King

Mark asked him.

Some of the nobles at Mark's court, who were jealous of Tristan, thought he would be sure to die if he went to King Gurman's court, and encouraged the king to send him. It was hard, indeed, for Tristan to go and ask for Iseult's hand for another man, and at the same time risk death. Yet he yearned to see Iseult again. So dressed this time as a merchant, he set out once more for Ireland. "At least if she marries King Mark I can be near her," he told himself.

Tristan had heard that since he had left Ireland a terrible dragon had come from its lair. It was laying waste lands with the fire that came from its mouth and eating so many people that no family felt safe. He knew that whoever killed the dragon would be able to ask a great favour from King Mark, and he planned to be that man. As soon as he set foot in Ireland all talk was of the dragon, and he had no difficulty in finding its lair for the land all around was burnt and blackened.

It takes courage and cleverness to kill a dragon, for swords and shields are melted in the fire it breathes, while a dragon's body is mostly covered in hard scales. As Tristan approached the dragon's lair he made up his mind that a sudden attack was his only chance, and so he rode up with his spear already levelled. The dragon, who awoke at the last moment, opened its jaws to spurt out flames, but in that split second Tristan's spear went into its mouth and buried itself in the back of its throat, inflicting great pain.

As the dragon whirled and roared, trying to dislodge the spear, Tristan's horse was killed beneath him, and now the young man attacked the dragon's scaly body on foot. It seemed he would be crushed beneath one of the dragon's great clawed feet, but Tristan plunged his sword through the soft skin on the dragon's underside, right into its heart. As the dragon fell dead, Tristan dragged himself clear. Then, pulling his sword free, he cut off the forked tip of the dragon's tongue and placed it in his pouch. The world was swimming around him as he staggered away, and he swooned and fell behind a rock.

Since Marhout, who had been the fiercest warrior in Ireland, was dead, King Gurman was in despair that he would never free his land

of the dragon. So he had proclaimed that whoever killed it could marry his daughter, the beautiful Iseult. The steward of his house longed to marry Iseult, and used to watch the dragon each night, trying to summon enough courage to attack it, yet knowing he could never succeed. He was both a coward and a poor swordsman. The evening that Tristan killed the dragon the steward came as usual to his watching-place, but to his surprise the dragon did not come out of its lair. Creeping up, he found its dead body, but no sign of the dragon-slayer. "I can claim victory for myself," he thought. He dipped his sword in the dragon's blood and he returned to court to announce that he had killed the dragon.

At once King Gurman sent men to establish that the dragon was dead, and then called his daughter and said, "Our steward has rid us of the dragon. I have promised him that you will be his bride."

Iseult could not bear the thought of marrying her father's steward, and knowing what a weak-hearted coward he was, she was convinced that he was lying. Desperate for some proof that might release her father from his promise, she went with her ladies and looked at the dragon for herself. There it lay, dead as the steward claimed. Then, behind the rock she saw a man lying, unconscious. Turning him over she found she was looking at her old love, the harpist who had disappeared from court many months before.

"There is a mystery here, which we must solve," she said, and she had Tristan carried back to the palace where she bathed his wounds and put ointment on his scorched skin. When she discovered, tucked into his pouch, the forked tip of the dragon's tongue, she knew the steward had not killed the dragon. Then her heart stood still for she saw the jagged edge to Tristan's sword. She took the fragment of metal she had kept since Marhout's death, and matched it against the sword. The harpist she loved was none other than Tristan, the killer of Marhout. And this was the man her father had sworn to kill.

Iseult went to her father and told him that the true dragon-slayer was the harpist who had stayed with them the previous year and that he was now recovering from the scorching he had received while fighting the dragon. So the next day King Gurman called the steward and Tristan to him and said, "One of you killed the dragon. Whoever it is shall have my daughter as wife. Now which of you is it to be?"

The steward spoke first. "How can you doubt my word, my lord, and how could a mere harpist kill a beast like that? You must believe me, your trusted steward."

Now Tristan stepped forward, and taking the forked tip of the dragon's tongue from his pouch, he said, "Here is my proof. Before I swooned from the heat of the dragon's breath, I cut off this." As they looked round the steward had disappeared, for he knew his lie had been uncovered.

"Then," said King Gurman, "although you are only a harpist, you shall have my daughter, Iseult, for your wife. I think she loves you already."

"There is something else I have to say," said Tristan. "I am, as you know, the man who came and played the harp at your court, and I am the man who slew the dragon, but I also am the man who killed your cousin Marhout."

"If this is true, then you must die, for I have sworn vengeance on he who killed Marhout. But his killer was Tristan of Cornwall, King Mark's nephew. How can this be?"

"I am Tristan, nephew of King Mark of Cornwall. The first time I came to your court it was to find a cure for my wound, for the sword that Marhout used had been dipped in poison. This was done, I believe by your wife, Iseult's mother, who has since died. I found the cure here, at the hands of your fair daughter, Iseult. Now I have come to ask that she return to Cornwall with me to marry King Mark. He dearly wants her as his wife."

"What, you do not seek her for yourself?" asked King Gurman.

"I seek her for my uncle," replied Tristan. As he spoke, Iseult, who had been gazing at him with love in her eyes, turned away in tears.

King Gurman looked at the young man for a long time, thinking deeply. "If Marhout fought with a poisoned sword, then I withdraw my promise of death to his killer, for he fought with dishonour. And the time has come for friendship between Ireland and Cornwall once more. I agree to send my daughter to be wife to King Mark, as you request," he said at last.

Word was sent ahead to King Mark, and preparations were made for Iseult to leave her home and travel with Tristan back to Cornwall. As the summer drew to a close the ship that was to take them was finally loaded and King Gurman rode to the port to bid his daughter farewell. For three days they sailed south-east on a fair wind, and then an autumn stillness came over the sea, and the ship was becalmed. Tristan ordered that he and Iseult should be put ashore on a small island while they waited for the wind to fill the ship's sails once more.

For two days Tristan and Iseult were happy beyond belief. Their love knew no bounds in this autumn idyll. They thought only of each other and their joy in being together, and ignored the shadow that hung over their happiness, the knowledge that soon Iseult was to be married to another man. On the third day, when a breeze ruffled the flat calm of the sea, they boarded their ship once more, pledged to each other and yet destined to live apart.

For several years they succeeded in this double life, for Tristan rode out on quests and adventures whenever he could, and Iseult tried to be happy with King Mark. But again and again they were drawn towards each other, until the word came to King Mark's ears that his wife loved another, and that other was his favourite nephew Tristan. Those who were still jealous of Tristan urged King Mark to put him to death, but the king chose to banish him. Now he wanders from place to place, looking for a new home, and a new king to serve.

* * *

Queen Guinevere, who understood so well the sadness of love, quietly put out her hand as the harpist concluded his tale. "And Tristan has come now to Camelot. Welcome, for we have long awaited you," she said gently.

"Welcome indeed," echoed King Arthur. "Your name is surely written at the Round Table where my knights gather. Come let us look together!" He was right, for there, beside Sir Lancelot's seat Sir Tristan's name had appeared, written in gold letters.

For many years Sir Tristan joined in the adventures and quests of the Knights of the Round Table. He was popular with them all, and

King Arthur was proud to have such a fine knight as one of his companions. In time Tristan married, and his bride was also called Iseult. She was not as beautiful as the lady he had given his heart to, but she was pretty and known to all as Iseult of the White Hands. He was as happy as he could be, and she adored him. She could not help, though, being jealous of her namesake who she knew was never far from the heart and mind of her husband.

Some years later, Sir Tristan was wounded by a spear. The wound festered and refused to heal, and as he lay on his sickbed Sir Tristan's mind turned always towards Iseult the Fair and her healing powers. At last, unable to think of any other way of staying alive, he sent Gorvenal, his old teacher, to Cornwall, requesting that Iseult the Fair should come and heal him. He instructed Gorvenal to return with a white sail on the boat if Iseult sailed with him, and a black sail if she did not.

Day after day he fretted and asked if the ship was in sight. Each time he asked, his wife's jealousy grew worse, until the day the ship was sighted. It carried a white sail, for Iseult had answered Sir Tristan's call for help and had sailed immediately with Gorvenal.

"Gorvenal's ship has rounded the cliffs and approaches the harbour," Iseult of the White Hands told her husband.

"And what colour is the sail?" he asked.

"The sail is black," she lied.

Tristan turned his face to the wall and spoke no other word. By the time Iseult and Gorvenal reached his bedside he had died. As she knelt by his dead body Iseult the Fair wept until she became ill, and then she too died, beside her true and dear love.

Iseult of the White Hands regretted her lie when she saw the depth of Tristan and Iseult's love for each other, but it was too late to bring them back to life. They were both buried in the same grave and over it she planted one white rose tree and one red. The roses from these trees entwined and grew together until they became one tree bearing both red and white roses. All who saw it recognised it as a symbol of their love.

13

LANCELOT AND ELAINE

Sir Lancelot was one of the bravest and most popular Knights of the Round Table. There are many stories of his adventures, when he brought honour and glory to the court of King Arthur. He was always anxious to fight on behalf of good people who were threatened by the wicked greed and jealousy of bad men, and his courage was famed far and wide. King Arthur was proud of Sir Lancelot and he was always welcomed with pleasure when he returned from one of his quests. There were times, though, when Lancelot rode out from Camelot because he could not bear to remain so close to Queen Guinevere, and yet not show his love for her.

One summer, several years after he had first come to Camelot, he rode far into the west, seeking adventure and hoping to put Queen Guinevere from his mind. He came in time to some desolate lands, where no plants grew well. Dead trees lay to either side of the track on which he rode, and the crops in the fields were shrivelled and stunted. Birds of prey hovered in the air, seeking the corpses of little animals who could not survive in this dry waste land. All around him there was an air of sadness.

On the horizon he saw a town with a tall tower. "Perhaps these people can tell me why so little lives in this area," he thought, as he rode towards it. As he entered the town many people approached and asked him if he had come to rescue the lady in the tower. "What lady is that, and why does she need rescuing?" he asked.

"She is the Lady Elaine, daughter of the King of Carbonek, who lives in the castle not far from here. She had a curse placed on her by Morgan le Fay, who was jealous, for Elaine is the most beautiful lady anyone has ever seen. She has been locked in the tower now for five years. All she knows of life is what she can see from the windows at the top of the tower. Only someone of great courage and goodness can release her from the curse. We have been told that this will be Sir Lancelot. Last year Sir Gawain tried, and failed.

"Where Gawain has failed, I have no chance of success," said Sir Lancelot, "but my name is Lancelot, and I cannot ride by without at least trying to help this unfortunate lady."

"Sir, they say if you break into the tower you will find her in a bath of boiling water, for that is part of the curse."

Sir Lancelot entered the door at the foot of the tower and climbed the steep staircase. He battered on the door at the top, and to his surprise the iron locks fell apart, and the door swung open. There in the room he saw a woman more beautiful than any he had seen before, except Queen Guinevere. She stood as naked as a needle in a great steaming bath, from which she said she could not come out. But when Sir Lancelot held out his hand she took it and found she was released from the spell. As she stepped onto the floor some ladies came with some robes for her.

Sir Lancelot waited below, and when Elaine was clothed and her hair combed, she came to join him. "Before we go to my father's house and tell him you have broken the spell that was laid on me, let us go to the chapel near here and give thanks for my release," she said.

At the chapel where they gave thanks Sir Lancelot was asked if he could now free them from the dragon that lurked beneath a tombstone there. Written on the tomb was:

HERE SHALL COME A LEOPARD OF KING'S BLOOD,
AND HE SHALL SLAY THIS SERPENT,
AND THIS LEOPARD SHALL ENGENDER A LION
IN THIS FOREIGN COUNTRY,
THE WHICH LION SHALL PASS ALL OTHER KNIGHTS.

Glad to have a challenge that tested his strength and wits, Sir Lancelot raised the tombstone, and from underneath rose up a huge and fierce dragon. Sir Lancelot took up his sword and shield and fought it. The dragon breathed fire and lashed out with its spiked tail. Sir Lancelot knew that if he fell he had no chance of staying alive. In the end, after fighting with all his wits and strength he was able to thrust his sword through the dragon's heart and it lay dead.

With great rejoicing for the death of the dragon and the release of the Lady Elaine, they rode through the waste lands to the castle of Carbonek, where Elaine's father greeted them. He could not come to the gates to welcome them for he still suffered from a wound he had received many years before, and had to lie on a couch. Now he shed tears of joy to see his daughter once more, and to hear the dragon was dead.

"Tell me why your castle is surrounded by waste lands," Lancelot asked. "Was it the dragon who caused this?"

"I am King Pelles, Lord of Carbonek. You may have heard that I received a wound, known as the Bitter Stroke, some years ago. I will never recover from it until the best knight in the world releases me. That knight is not yet born, but now you have killed the dragon, if the ancient prophecy on the tombstone is to come true, it will be your son who will save me from my suffering."

"But I have no son," said Lancelot.

"Before long I hope that will change," said King Pelles, "but let us talk later. You should now prepare yourself for a meal, as we eat soon. A room awaits you. You will remain here for several days as a guest of honour, Sir Lancelot.

Lancelot remembered tales of King Pelles and the waste lands around his castle of Carbonek and decided to ask his host more about it as they ate their meal. But as they sat down at the high table something happened that put all other thoughts out of his mind.

A dove seemed to hover in the light of a western window, and then, almost as though Lancelot saw it in a dream, the table was covered in food and drink. Still dazzled, he then saw a young girl dressed in white and with long flowing hair enter the hall. Between her hands she carried a golden cup of great beauty. She walked, or rather she seemed to float, round the hall, and all those she passed bowed their heads. Then, in silence, still bearing the cup, she glided out of the hall.

"Who was that, and why does she carry that cup?" Lancelot asked.

"You should know, Lancelot, that I am a descendant of Joseph of Arimathea. He it was who offered his tomb for the burial of Jesus Christ. That cup you saw just now is none other than the Holy Grail, the cup that was used at the Last Supper, the night before Jesus was crucified. It is also the cup which caught the drops of blood as Jesus hung on the cross. Joseph of Arimathea often came to this country to trade, and when he was an old man he lived here. He brought the Holy Grail with him. My family has been the keepers of it over the centuries. This most holy object will one day go from here to King Arthur's court at Camelot. We await the finest knight of all time to take it there. When this happens, the curse on my lands will be removed, and the wound which has troubled me and kept me on a couch for many years will finally be healed."

Lancelot listened and wondered at what King Pelles said, for he had heard elsewhere that the Holy Grail would go to Camelot with one of the Knights of the Round Table. The name of that knight was not yet written in gold on the table but a seat awaited him. It was called the Seat of Danger. King Pelles saw the thoughtful look in Lancelot's eyes, and said, "Part of the prophecy is that the Holy Grail will go to Camelot only when King Arthur's power is nearly over. When it leaves this place, the fellowship of the Knights of the Round Table will soon come to an end."

King Pelles did not comment on that other prophecy, the one written on the tombstone: he who killed the dragon would be father of the greatest knight of them all. But he knew that Lancelot's son would be the greatest knight. Only when he was born and grown to be a man would he, King Pelles, be released from the torment of the wound which kept him on his couch day and night. He looked at his lovely daughter, Elaine, free at last from her tower, and saw how she gazed at Sir Lancelot with love. "These two will be the parents of the knight who will come for the Holy Grail," he thought, "and she is so beautiful, he will soon love her as she loves him."

So King Pelles persuaded Sir Lancelot to stay with him in Carbonek for many days, and arranged for Elaine to play chess with him and ride out in the forest with him. Each day she loved him more, and yet he never really thought about her for all his thoughts were still with Queen Guinevere.

At last King Pelles called Bryssen, Elaine's old nurse to him, and said, "If Sir Lancelot does not himself think of marrying Elaine, how are we do make him do so? She loves him, and he will never find a more beautiful bride. We all await the birth of Lancelot's son, Galahad. How can we help them come together so he will be born?"

"Leave it to me," Bryssen assured him. "I will use my knowledge of potions and medicines to make sure that Sir Lancelot will love your daughter. He only thinks of Queen Guinevere now, but I will open his eyes for him to see the true beauty of Elaine."

Bryssen persuaded Elaine to go to another castle owned by her father, called the castle of Case. "Lancelot will come to you there," she told her. She went with Elaine and prepared everything with great care and in the evening she sent her husband back to Carbonek with a ring that looked like the ring Queen Guinevere always wore.

"The lady sends this ring, and asks you to join her," Bryssen's husband said to Sir Lancelot.

Sir Lancelot, who had been day-dreaming of Guinevere, thought at once that it was her ring. "Where is she?" he asked urgently.

"She awaits you in a castle nearby. I will lead you there."

So Lancelot hurried with Bryssen's husband through the waste lands. "Where is she?" he asked again, as he rode into the courtyard.

"She is tired and has gone to her bedroom already," the old nurse said. "Come, my lord, and have a drink before you join her."

So Lancelot sat by the fire and drank a cup of wine that had been prepared for him. It had special herbs infused in it that would confuse his mind. Then, in the darkness, he slipped into the bedroom where Elaine waited.

As early sunlight streamed through the window the next morning, Sir Lancelot turned on his elbow and gazed at the lady next to him. When he saw it was not Guinevere he jumped from the bed and seized his sword, shouting with rage.

Elaine, frightened that Lancelot would kill her, went on her knees and begged for her life. "I have only done this because I love you so dearly. And it was necessary for us to conceive a son, so that he may grow to be the finest knight and take the Holy Grail to Camelot. Our son will do this and more, for he will cure my father from the wound he has suffered from for so many years, and the waste lands around here will grow green again. Come, my love, forgive me."

"I can forgive you, but I can never forgive myself," said Sir Lancelot in anguish. His eyes blazed with madness for the pain he felt overwhelmed him, and he jumped from the window as he was, clothed only in his shirt. He fell into a bush of roses and tearing himself free, he fled into the waste lands.

* * *

For over a year no one heard from Sir Lancelot, and in Camelot they grew anxious. When he missed the great Whitsun feast several of his friends rode out to ask around the country if he had been seen anywhere. Sir Bors eventually came to the castle of Carbonek, and was invited to stay awhile by King Pelles. There he met Elaine, who carried a baby boy in her arms. The infant opened his eyes wide as Sir Bors leant over him, and Sir Bors saw the eyes of Sir Lancelot staring up at him. Startled, he looked at Elaine, who said, "Yes, Sir Lancelot was here, and this is his son. He is called Galahad. One day he shall become the greatest knight of all time. But I do not know where his father is, for he went off into the waste lands and has not been seen for many months."

When Sir Bors returned to Camelot he told them all he knew, that Sir Lancelot had been in Carbonek, and that he and the Lady Elaine had a son called Galahad. When this news came to Queen Guinevere's ears she burnt with jealousy and she longed even more to see Lancelot. But no word came for two more years of Sir Lancelot.

One day, at the castle of Case, where Elaine lived with her young son Galahad, the boy came running to her and said a wild man lay asleep in the bushes near the well. She went with him, and there she found Sir Lancelot, lying by the well. He was covered in wounds and scratches, and looked as though he had been living rough for many months. Her old nurse Bryssen came out, and together they moved

Sir Lancelot to a room in the castle. When he awoke, the madness had gone from his eyes, and he lay back on the pillows weak and exhausted.

For several weeks he stayed there recovering his strength. He could recall little or nothing of his time in the forest where he had lived like an animal, sleeping in a cave and eating only berries and fruits. But he remembered Elaine and his own betrayal of Guinevere, and as he grew stronger he longed to return to Camelot. He never once asked to see his son, Galahad. Elaine tried to keep him with her, hoping he would marry her, but when his strength returned he asked for a horse and he rode away.

In Camelot, he was given a great welcome. They had heard that he had become crazy and had been living wild in the forest, and they were delighted to see he was his old self once more. Only Queen Guinevere turned away when he looked at her, and refused to smile into his eyes as she had always done before.

At last they were able to talk alone, and Lancelot told her the whole story, of how he had rescued Elaine from the tower, killed the dragon and stayed on in the castle of Carbonek with King Pelles. Then he told her how he had been tricked by the nurse Bryssen and how he had thought he had lain with Guinevere that night. ''I only went there because of my love for you,'' he said. As they looked at each other their old passion flared up even more strongly than before, and Guinevere forgave him.

* * *

For some years Elaine cared for Galahad, but she knew she was ill and had not long to live. She took the boy to an abbey, and instructed the holy men to care for him until he was fifteen and then to send him to King Arthur's court at Camelot. She then wrote a letter and filled a barge with flowers and had it draped in black. Dressed in her finest gown she lay in the barge among the flowers. A dumb man was told to steer the barge up the river to Camelot.

So it was that one day King Arthur and Guinevere were looking over the walls of their palace in Camelot, down onto the river, and

King Arthur noticed a strange boat draped in black, being poled along. He called for Sir Kay, his steward, and sent him to see what it held.

Sir Kay returned and said, "The barge is steered by a man who cannot speak, and inside lies a lady as fair as any ever seen. She lies on a bed of flowers and I think she is dying or already dead."

Now Arthur and Guinevere came down to the river's edge, followed by a crowd of curious onlookers. Gently they took the letter that was held in Elaine's hands as she lay there, still and quiet. King Arthur started to read the letter aloud, and then he stopped and handed it to Sir Lancelot for it was addressed to him.

The letter said, "Most noble Lancelot, now death has taken my love from you, but know since I first met you, my heart has been yours. Give me now a decent burial, and pray for my soul."

Lancelot bowed his head with shame as he saw the lady Elaine, who had loved him so dearly and who had born his son. He knew he had treated her shamefully, and now she was dead he could never ask her forgiveness, nor explain that he felt it wrong to marry her when he could not love her.

"Come," said King Arthur kindly, "we will give this lady who loved you so much a resting place within the burial ground of Camelot and we will pray for her. Love has its own ways, and cannot be tamed."

So the lady Elaine was buried with splendour in Camelot. Sir Lancelot grieved, not for her, but that he had behaved badly towards her. And all the time his love for Guinevere grew even stronger, and hers for him, so fulfilling Merlin's foreboding that King Arthur's marriage to Guinevere would bring harm and even destruction to the Knights of the Round Table.

14

THE MARRIAGE OF SIR GAWAIN

One of the best loved of all the tales of King Arthur and the Knights of the Round Table is the story of Sir Gawain's marriage, for it is a story that tells of battles and trickery, of love and riddles and of magic.

It began one winter when King Arthur, who had now been king for many years, had taken his court to the north for the Christmas and New Year celebrations. Queen Guinevere and many of the knights were there with him to enjoy the feasting and hunting.

One afternoon, as dusk was closing in, a lady rode up to King Arthur's palace. She said that the day before her lord had been lured into a dark and fearsome castle by a wicked knight called The Knight of Tarn Witherlane. When she had tried to prevent this, the monstrous knight, who was said to have magic powers, had beaten her about the face. She had red weals across her cheek to prove her story.

"I come to ask for your help," she said to King Arthur. "Please help me to rescue my lord."

"I will go myself, tomorrow, at first light," King Arthur announced.

At once there was a clamour from many of the knights who said, "You should not go, Arthur! You are high king! There might be danger. One of us must go."

"What, am I to be protected from all danger?" asked King Arthur, angrily. "I should not like to be thought too old or weak for such adventures. I shall go and challenge the Knight of Tarn Witherlane myself, since this lady came to me for help."

It was a bleak winter's morning as King Arthur rode out through the forest of Inglewood with only the lady to show the way, and a squire for company. After some hours they came out of the forest and on to desolate moorland. Great boulders lay strewn around a lake which shone dark under the metal-coloured sky. Beyond the lake stood a towering black castle. A sense of evil magic seemed to hang in the air.

"This is where we were attacked, yesterday," the lady said, "and it was into that castle that my lord was dragged by the Knight of Tarn Witherlane."

King Arthur took the hunting horn that hung from his saddle and blew a blast. Immediately a great knight rode out of the castle.

"Why, if it's not King Arthur himself," he called out. "I shall be glad to fight you, for I have long wanted your kingdom, and now I shall have it!"

"Fight you shall," shouted back King Arthur, "for I have come to release the knight you took as prisoner yesterday! And you struck this lady in the face. I cannot allow you to dishonour a lady in this way."

Arthur lowered his helmet and raised his spear, ready to fight. He heard the Knight of Tarn Witherlane laugh, which heightened his anger. Then, as he charged towards the castle he felt the unbelievable happen. His horse stopped so suddenly that Arthur nearly fell off, and his spear wobbled and fell useless in his hand. The squire saw all this and confirmed that the king was speaking the truth when he said he was unable to fight. Some magic power held him in its grip and it was impossible for him to attack. The squire also reported that the lady who had led them there, slipped away with a smile on her face. Her task as messenger had been completed. King Arthur had ridden straight into a trap.

"I see King Arthur is not so mighty as he thinks," roared the Knight of Tarn Witherlane. Do you agree to hand me your kingdom?"

"Certainly not!" replied King Arthur angrily.

"Well, if you cannot fight me with arms, perhaps you can show me how clever you are. If I ask you a riddle and you fail to bring me the answer within one year, I will slay you here outside my castle and throw your body into this cold dark lake. I shall also declare to all that

I have taken over your kingship.''

''You have only to ask the question,'' said Arthur, ''and I shall bring you the answer.''

''You must swear that you will return, and on your own,'' said the knight.

''You have my word of honour. I am King Arthur. I shall return with the answer as you ask,'' said the king.

''The question is simple: 'What do women desire above all else?' You may not find the answer so easy,'' called out the Knight of Tarn Witherlane.

''Never doubt, I shall return with it,'' replied King Arthur.

''I'm sure we will find the correct answer to this riddle,'' Arthur said to his squire as they rode back through the forest, but he was already worried, for he knew that women desire many things. How was he to name the one thing they want above all others?

The Knights of the Round Table were sympathetic to Arthur's predicament, for they had heard that magic hung over the black castle by the lake. Besides, everyone loved to try and answer riddles. Each person at King Arthur's court had their own suggestions for the answer to this one: pretty clothes, lovely jewellery, happiness, love, beauty, comfort, long life. These and many other ideas were put forward.

Sir Gawain offered to ride around the kingdom asking the question of all the women he met. The list of things that women desire grew and grew, and Gawain filled two books with all the answers he was given throughout the year.

By the following Christmas, King Arthur was not convinced he had the right answer, but he rode to keep his appointment with the Knight of Tarn Witherlane. Sir Gawain rode with him for part of the way. As they approached the desolate spot near the dark and magic lake, they came across a woman riding alone in the forest. She was dressed in fine clothes, but as they drew near they flinched and looked away, for she was the ugliest woman they had ever seen. She had warts on her face, her eyes looked in two directions at once, and her skin was pitted with hideous marks. When she called them over they saw all her teeth were broken and black, and her voice was

cracked and rasping.

"You ride to your death, King Arthur. I know you have sought far and wide for the answer to the riddle, but I do not believe you have found it yet. Come nearer and I will whisper the correct answer in your ear."

King Arthur hesitated, reluctant to go near such an ugly person. "Why should you help me?" he asked.

"If I don't help you, you will die today. In return for saving your life, I want something from you," she croaked.

"What can I give you?" asked King Arthur.

"A promise that this day I shall wed a knight of noble birth."

"That I cannot promise," said Arthur quickly. "I am not free to marry you myself, nor can I pledge another man to marry without his consent."

Now Gawain came forward. "I shall marry this lady. We can be wed today after you have delivered the correct answer to the riddle. It is better by far that you should live and continue to be our king than you should be destroyed by the Knight of Tarn Witherlane."

"I cannot ask you to do this for me," Arthur protested, looking at the ugly lady again.

"But I wish to marry her, for all our sakes," swore Gawain.

So the ugly lady drew King Arthur towards her and whispered something in his ear. At once the king smiled for he knew she had the true answer to the riddle. Now he rode on alone to keep his word and deliver the message.

As he approached the castle, the gates opened and the huge knight rode out. "Ah! We have the king who could not fight me. Now he comes to tell me he does not know the answer to my question. I hope you are prepared for death, King Arthur. I can assure you I look forward to becoming high king before this day is out."

"Here are some answers to your question," called out King Arthur, and he took the lists that Gawain had prepared and read out one answer after another.

The knight's loud and cruel laughter echoed round the lake. Not one of those is right," he shouted. "Now ride over here and prepare for death!"

120

"I have one more answer," called out the king. Slowly, looking the Knight of Tarn Witherlane firmly in the eye, he said, "What every woman wants above all else is to have her own way."

There was a shriek of rage from the knight. "Who gave you that answer?"

"A hideous woman we met on the way!"

"That is my sister Ragnell. She has betrayed me." And the knight turned and rode into the castle, leaving Arthur to ride back and join Gawain and his promised bride.

As they rode back to where the court was staying, Arthur went ahead to announce that the wedding of Gawain, his favourite nephew, would take place that day. Many people gathered at the gates of the town to see Gawain and his lady ride in. Their smiles of pleasure, for Gawain was popular, turned to gasps of shock and dismay when they saw the hideous lady riding beside him. Gawain ignored them all, and led the lady first to the palace, and then to the church where the wedding ceremony took place.

At the feast that evening men and women found it hard to look at Gawain's bride, while at the same time they found themselves staring in fascinated horror. They could not believe that Gawain could have married anyone so ugly.

As they retired to their bedroom, Gawain wondered how they would pass the night. He knew he had to stay with his bride on this their wedding night. If he did not do so, word would get back to the Knight of Tarn Witherlane who would come and claim the life of King Arthur.

"Will you not kiss me, my lord?" asked the ugly lady when they were alone.

Gawain reluctantly took her in his arms and kissed her. Then he turned away from her terrible face.

"Can you not bear to look at me, my lord?" she said in a different voice.

Gawain made himself turn once more towards her.

There, standing before him was the loveliest lady he had ever seen. Her hair was long and golden, her skin was smooth and her teeth were white as milk. She held her arms towards him.

"You have broken the spell! Thank you a thousand times."

"What spell?"

"Morgan le Fay, the king's sister, put an enchantment on my brother and me. His task was to lure the king to a certain death. Mine was to remain ugly until a knight from a noble family married me. She did not think that any knight would ever do so. I feared I would pass the whole of my life as you found me, ugly and repulsive."

Tears of happiness fell down her beautiful face, and Gawain kissed them away. "No more sorrow, now, my love," he said. "King Arthur lives and I have married a lovely lady."

"One half of the enchantment remains," she said, sadly. "I am only partly released from my ugliness. I can be as you see me now by day or by night. You must choose whether you want me to be beautiful by day and ugly by night, or the other way round."

Gawain paused to think. "If I have you to myself, lovely as you are, each night, how wonderful it will be for me. But how dreadful for you, each day, to join the queen and the other ladies of the court in your ugly form."

The Lady Ragnell hung her head and waited for Gawain to go on.

"But if I choose to let you spend the day in all your beauty, how hard it will be for us each night."

Still the Lady Ragnell hung her head and waited.

"I do not know, my love, which to choose. Since it affects you more than anyone, the choice must be yours."

At once Ragnell's arms were around his neck, and she looked at Gawain with joy. "You have said the only thing that could release me completely from the spell. You have allowed me to have my own way! Now I need never return to being ugly. Oh, Gawain, did you know the answer to the riddle that I whispered to King Arthur this morning? 'What every woman wants most is to have her own way!' I never dreamed that such a knight as you would break the spell completely by giving me my own way."

Gawain and Ragnell appeared the next morning and told Arthur and Guinevere of their happiness in being together. They talked of the enchantment which Arthur's wicked sister had placed on her and her brother, and how Gawain, by letting Ragnell have her own way had broken the spell. Her brother, too, she said would now be released from the enchantment that Morgan le Fay had placed on him.

For seven years Sir Gawain found great happiness with Ragnell. Their marriage was full of love and joy. But then, one day, she disappeared. No one knew where she went. Some said it was to the forests of Wales, others thought she went even further away. There were some who hinted that she had come from the distant under-world of magic, and no more than seven years were allowed to her as a mortal before she had to return. Whatever it was that drove her away from Gawain, he was left grieving, for he had loved her dearly.

15

PERCIVAL AND BLANCHEFLEUR

Throughout his childhood, Percival lived with his mother in the forests of Wales. He dressed in animal skins, and ran lightfooted as a deer through the trees. With one of his own weapons, a sharp-pointed dart, he could bring down a bird or kill an animal more swiftly than most hunters using a bow and arrow. He knew nothing of the world outside his part of the forest. This upbringing made Percival different from other men.

One day when Percival was fifteen, he heard the jingle of horses' bits and the murmur of men's voices as they rode down one of the forest tracks. He crept up through the trees, until he could see five knights riding by. He gasped with amazement, for he had never seen a knight before. Sir Lancelot, who rode at the head of the group and who always had a quick and keen eye, caught a glimpse of the wild looking youth peering from behind a tree. "Come here, boy," he called, "and tell us why you are following us?"

"I only wonder who you are, for I have never seen your like before. Are you God's angels?" said Percival.

"We are certainly not angels," the knights laughed. One then added kindly, "We serve God as the angels do, but our earthly master is King Arthur. We are Knights of the Round Table."

"How could I become a knight?"

"You should come and ask King Arthur to make you one," came the reply, and with another laugh the knights rode on.

Percival ran as fast as he could back to the hut where he lived. "Mother," he said, "I have seen five knights today. I thought they were angels, but they tell me they serve King Arthur. I want to be like them. I must ride to find King Arthur. They told me that is what I must do if I am to become a knight.''

''Then you will soon see angels, my son. Your father and your uncles were all knights. I feared you would become one too, only to ride off to fight and to die like they did. That's why I have kept you here in the forest all these years. You should stay here with me now, and forget the world of knights.''

''But I must go, Mother,'' young Percival cried, ''and I must go quickly, or I shall not be able to follow the knights and find the way to King Arthur.''

His mother's tears fell as she helped Percival gather together his few belongings. As she placed some freshly baked honey cakes in his pouch, he snatched up some of the darts he used when he was hunting. Then he turned to bid his mother farewell.

''Take this ring, Percival, which belonged to your father,'' she said, and she placed on his finger a golden ring set with a shining diamond. ''Remember always to come to the aid of any woman or girl who seeks help. You may take a kiss from a maiden, but only if she gives it willingly. Otherwise take nothing, unless it is a ring which you should exchange with a ring of your own. And remember, my son, to honour God always. You should never pass a church or chapel without praying.''

Percival found there were tears in his own eyes as he walked away from his mother and his home, but before long he picked up the marks of the horses' hooves in the forest track and his heart filled with joy and excitement at the thought of becoming a knight. He followed the trail, not knowing how long it would take him to reach King Arthur's court.

Towards evening he came to a glade in the forest where a building stood that was larger and more grand than any Percival had seen before. ''Is this a church or chapel?'' he asked himself, and entered the door, prepared to pray as his mother had told him. But this was no church. Before him, sleeping on silken couch lay a beautiful girl. Percival gazed at her, then leant and kissed her on the lips. Mindful of his mother's instructions, he placed the diamond ring from his own hand on her finger, and took from her finger a ring which glistened with a deep red ruby. Then, fearful that she should wake and he would not know what to do, he crept out.

Percival slept deep in the forest, and journeyed on next morning. By midday he could see a castle ahead of him. He wondered at its size, but he never hesitated for he saw knights riding out and others riding in. Above all else he felt the urge to join them and so he walked on through the town and into the castle. As he entered the hall he gazed in excitement at the scene before him. It was Easter, and many were gathered for a feast. The king sat on a dais at the end of the hall and with him sat Sir Lancelot and the other knights he had met in the forest. Down the length of the hall were more tables with more knights. Dogs crouched beneath the tables hoping for scraps, and serving men ran to and fro with cups of silver and gold and with platters laden with meat and bread.

As Percival stood just inside the door gazing at everything a tall man in red-gold armour strode in, disturbing everyone. With no hesitation he marched to the high table where King Arthur sat, and seized the jewelled and golden goblet from which the king was about to drink. He then walked down the length of the hall, stuffing the goblet in his pouch. There was an outcry, and King Arthur leapt to his feet. "We must get that cup back, and quickly! What a ruffian that man is, for all that he wears fine armour."

"Let me go, let me go," came many cries, but King Arthur said, "Such a man is not a worthy foe for a Knight of the Round Table. Let some squire who is yet to prove his valour take on this quest."

Immediately Percival called out, "Let me go, King Arthur. I will fetch back your cup."

"Who is this woodsman's son?" sneered Sir Kay.

"My name is Percival, and I long above all else to become a Knight of the Round Table!"

Now Sir Lancelot recognised the boy he had met in the forest, and told the king of their encounter.

"You shall be provided with horse and armour. Fetch back my cup if you can, Percival," said the king, " Then we will see whether you shall be a knight or not."

"Provide me with a horse," replied young Percival, "But let me

win my armour from the man I go to fight."

"Well spoken, brave knight," called out a girl in the hall.

"He is no knight nor will he ever be one, " snarled Sir Kay, and slapped the girl to silence her.

"I shall punish you for that when I return," called out Percival, as he hurried from the hall to find a horse.

"That young woodsman will bring more glory to this court than you ever will", said the girl, glaring at Sir Kay.

Percival rode as fast as he could after the stranger in red-gold armour. At last, as they were climbing a steep hill, he came within earshot.

"Halt there, cup-stealer!" called out Percival. "I have come to fetch back the goblet you have just stolen from King Arthur."

The stranger stopped and glared at the boy in animal skins who rode behind him. "I take instructions from no man, least of all an insolent youth dressed like a wild animal. You shall be punished for your insolence!" And with this the knight turned, levelled his spear into a fighting position and charged downhill towards Percival. In the last moment Percival leapt from his horse and the spear whistled through empty air.

"So," called out Percival, as the knight attempted to pull up his horse as it galloped down the hill, "you attack unarmed men as well as being a thief."

The stranger turned and rode back up the hill. He was red in the face with rage, and he levelled his spear once more at the boy who was now jumping up and down on the ground, taunting him. As he charged, Percival leapt aside and threw one of his darts. It flew straight and true, and caught his enemy where there was a join in his armour. With a terrible cry of pain and rage the knight in red-gold armour fell to the ground, and within very few minutes he was dead.

Percival stooped to take the goblet from the dead man's pouch, and then he decided to take off his armour. "It's what I told King Arthur I would do," he said to himself. Since he knew nothing of armour, he did not know where or how it fastened, and he could not see how to get the dead man out of it.

"Can I help you?" a kindly voice enquired. Percival saw an old knight smiling down at him.

"I have killed this man who stole a goblet from King Arthur," Percival explained, "and now I need his armour, so I can return and ask the king if he will make me a knight."

"There is more to becoming a knight than killing a man. May I suggest you return to my house while I teach you many of the skills you need to become a knight. My name is Sir Gonemans, and my home is not far away. I will treat you as a son and teach you all I know."

Percival watched the old man's fingers deftly remove the red-gold armour from the dead man, and then with guidance, he put it on himself. He placed the goblet safely in his own pouch and rode with Gonemans to an ancient manor house.

He stayed throughout the summer, learning how to fight with a sword and a spear, how to carry a shield, how to wear armour and much more besides. He was a keen and adept pupil, and Gonemans was proud to instruct such a fine young man. "King Arthur will be glad to have him," he often thought to himself.

As summer turned to autumn Percival thanked the old man, and set out towards Camelot. His eyes sometimes strayed to the ruby ring on his finger and he wondered if he would ever again find the beautiful girl he had kissed the day he left home. He rode for many days, uncertain which road to take for Camelot, and came in time to some desolate waste lands. Far ahead he could see a castle.

Lights shone from the windows and Percival rode boldly into the courtyard, although he could see no other sign of life. He left his horse in the stable and climbed the stairs to the hall, where the lights were lit. There before a fire stood a chessboard, set out for a game. Percival had played many games of chess with Sir Gonemans, so he idly moved a white pawn, making the opening move. Instantly one of the red pieces moved, although no hand touched it. "Truly this is a place full of magic," said Percival to himself, as he moved another white chessman. Again a red piece was moved through some invisible force. In very few moves Percival was defeated. He played two more games with his invisible opponent, and each time he was the loser. Suddenly Percival lost patience, and raised his fist to smash the board when a girl appeared, and placed a restraining hand on his arm.

Percival looked up at her. The diamond ring on her finger caught the light as she moved her arm. "Who are you?" he asked.

"I am Blanchefleur," she replied, and she stood very still as she saw the ruby ring on his hand.

"I have been searching for you, Blanchefleur, for I kissed you one evening as you lay asleep. I knew no better then, but it was wrong of me. For this I apologise. You wear my ring, and I wear yours. Again, I should not have made this exchange without first asking you. My name is Percival."

"Oh, Percival, I saw you in my dreams the night you gave me the kiss and exchanged rings. I have longed to see you again, but while I am awake, not just in my dreams. You have been brought to this castle of Carbonek in the waste lands for a purpose. Let us go to the table for a meal, for there is something you must see."

There was no food on the table, nor was there sign of any servants to bring it. Then a great sound of thunder echoed throughout the hall, and Percival watched as a strange procession approached. First came a girl wearing a long white robe. She carried a cup, holding it high before her, and from the cup a light shone which dazzled Percival, making him shield his eyes. Then came another maiden carrying a heavy candlestick with seven great burning candles. Behind her followed a third maiden with a spear which she held before her. From it dripped scarlet drops of blood, yet none fell on the floor. Percival knelt with Blanchefleur as the procession passed.

When they were alone once more in the hall, he turned and saw the table was laid with a magnificent spread.

"You are one of the few to see the Holy Grail," Blanchefleur said to him. "It is the cup from which Jesus Christ drank at the last supper. The spear is the same one used to pierce his side when he was crucified. Joseph of Arimathea who gave his tomb for Jesus' burial, brought these precious objects to Britain. He lived here when he was an old man, and some say he is the ancestor of the maimed King, King Pelles, who lies upstairs. He suffers from an old wound."

As they ate, Percival thought of what Blanchefleur had told him, but even more he thought of how beautiful she was. "Will you be my wife, Blanchefleur?" he eventually asked. "I could never love anyone but you."

"I may not marry until the Holy Grail has a new keeper. Many will seek it but only one knight will reach it, and that time has not yet come, Percival."

With a cry of grief, for he could not see how he could live without her, Percival sprang from the table, and ran from the castle. He took his horse from the stable and rode out into the waste lands. The next day, when he tried to return to Carbonek he could not find the castle. With a great sadness in his heart for having lost Blanchefleur a second time, he rode on to find King Arthur.

* * *

His thoughts were still with the beautiful Blanchefleur, even as he approached Camelot. He had reined in his horse and was sitting deep in thought, gazing into the distance, and did not notice a group of knights approaching.

"Who is that knight in fine armour? I don't recognise him," said King Arthur, who was with the knights.

"We'll soon find out," said Sir Kay, and he called out, "Ho there! Tell us who you are and why you ride this way."

When he received no answer from the young man day-dreaming on his horse, Sir Kay rode up and slapped him across the face with his gauntlet. "Let that teach you some manners," he said.

"Perhaps this will teach you some manners," replied Percival who had been startled by Sir Kay's rude approach, and he turned and raised his spear. The two rode against each other, and in very few minutes Sir Kay was on the ground."

Now Sir Gawain came up to Percival. "Are you not the young man who rode out on the quest to recover the goblet stolen from King Arthur at Easter?"

"I am. My name is Percival. I am riding to Camelot to return the cup to King Arthur. I have it here. I am hoping that he will then make me a knight. I also seek out Sir Kay, for I owe him a blow for hitting the girl who called out encouragement to me on that day.''

''That is Sir Kay, there on the ground. You have already given him the blow he deserves. And here is King Arthur.''

Percival leapt from his horse and knelt before the king, holding out the goblet he had been carrying. ''Lord King, I have recovered your cup and gained myself some armour. I have also learnt many of the things a knight should know from a wise teacher. May I join the Knights of the Round Table?''

''Kneel, Percival, and you shall gain your knighthood now,'' said King Arthur. Then he touched him on both shoulders with a sword and said, ''Arise Sir Percival!''

As Percival rose to his feet, the king said, ''I have waited many years for you, Sir Percival. When the Round Table first came to Camelot, Merlin advised me that a young knight called Percival would sit next to the Seat of Danger. Let us go and see if your name is now written at your place.''

Percival's name was indeed written in letters of gleaming gold at the place between Sir Gawain and the Seat of Danger.

''We await only one more knight, and then my table will be complete,'' King Arthur said. ''Merlin's prophecy was that you and he, the last two to join us, will bring great glory to the fellowship of the Round Table. Welcome, Sir Percival!''

16

SIR GALAHAD COMES TO CAMELOT

The Knights of the Round Table were gathering in Camelot for the Whitsun feast. It was many years now since King Arthur had founded the order of the Knights of the Round Table, and some wondered whether there were any adventures still to come. Heads turned as a young lady rode in the courtyard. Her horse's hooves clattered over the stones in the gateway and it stood there lathered in sweat and with heaving flanks for she had ridden in great haste. "I seek Sir Lancelot," she said to the guards.

When Sir Lancelot came, she said most urgently, "King Pelles bids me bring you with me to an abbey in the forest. The reason will be explained when you are there."

"Madam, I will come at once," replied Sir Lancelot.

Queen Guinevere came to see what was causing the disturbance. On hearing that Lancelot was to ride out of Camelot, she protested. "Tomorrow is our Whitsun feast. You cannot go away today of all days."

The young lady who had ridden for Lancelot laid a hand on the queen's arm. "Sir Lancelot will be back with you tomorrow in time to celebrate with you here in Camelot."

"If that is the case," said the queen, "I will not complain any more at his going."

Sir Lancelot was full of curiosity when they came to the abbey. He was led to the guest chamber, where his sword and shield were taken from him. To his surprise and joy he found his cousins, Sir Bors and Sir Lionel were already there.

"Lancelot, what are you doing here?" they called out. "We're on our way to Camelot and we expected to find you there."

"I shall be returning to Camelot tomorrow in time for the feast. The full reason for being here is not yet clear. All I know is that King Pelles, who lies sick at the castle of Carbonek, has requested it."

As they talked, twelve nuns came into the room leading a young man. "Sir," they said to Lancelot, "we bring this young man to you, for he is ready to become a knight, and it is King Pelles' wish that he should be knighted by you. We know of no more worthy man to receive knighthood. He has all the qualities such an honour deserves."

Sir Lancelot saw a fine looking youth. "Come forward young man, and tell me your name and if it is your wish to become a knight," he said.

"My name is Galahad, and I wish it above all else."

Now Sir Lancelot knew why King Pelles had sent for him. The young man standing before him was his own son. His mother was dead, and King Pelles was his grandfather. He said to Galahad, "Tomorrow is the feast of Whitsun. I propose that you kneel in vigil tonight in the chapel here, and tomorrow I shall make you a knight. But you will need armour."

"I will get my armour after I become a knight," the young man replied. It was with pride that Sir Lancelot looked at his son. He was glad to see him after so many years, and he was delighted he had been invited to confer knighthood upon him.

Galahad stayed all night before the abbey altar. The next morning he knelt before Sir Lancelot, who touched him on either shoulder with his sword, saying, "Arise, Sir Galahad."

"Now I ride to Camelot to take my place at the Whitsun feast with King Arthur and Queen Guinevere. Sir Bors and Sir Lionel, both Knights of the Round Table, ride with me. Will you come with us?" he said to Galahad.

"I will come to King Arthur's court in my own time," replied the young man.

At Camelot, Lancelot found many of the knights who were to attend the feast looking at their names at the Round Table. Every place except one had a knight's name written in gold letters. In all the years since the Round Table had come to Camelot, the Seat of Danger had never had a name by it. But now Sir Lancelot, who sat next to it, saw something written there. He read the words:

THIS SEAT SHALL BE FILLED IN THE YEAR
FOUR HUNDRED AND FIFTY FOUR.

"I think the knight who is to sit here will come today," said Lancelot, "for it is four hundred and fifty-four years since Jesus Christ was hung on the cross. Let us cover this place with a cloth of silk until the knight arrives."

After a service in the church the knights took their seats at the table. Only the Seat of Danger, still covered with a silken cloth, remained empty. They were about to start the feast when Sir Kay called out, "King Arthur, have you forgotten our custom? We never begin until some adventure or strange happening has taken place."

King Arthur replied, "You are right, Sir Kay. I was so overjoyed to see Sir Lancelot had returned in time for the feast, bringing his cousins with him, that I forgot our old custom. We will wait and see if any adventure or quest presents itself."

Even as he spoke a squire came running into the hall. "Sir," he said to King Arthur, "a strange stone has appeared floating on the river, and in the stone there is a sword!"

"We must go and look at this marvel," said King Arthur, and he led the Knights of the Round Table down to the river bank. He remembered how he had pulled his own sword from the stone in the churchyard when he had been a boy of fifteen, and how later he had taken his sword, called Excalibur, from the hand that held it above the lake. Now they all saw what looked like a slab of red marble floating on the water. From it arose a sword standing up like a golden cross. Its hilt was studded with glistening jewels and precious stones, and on the sword blade was written:

NO MAN MAY TAKE ME EXCEPT THE TRUE OWNER,
AND HE SHALL BE THE BEST KNIGHT IN ALL THE WORLD.

When the king saw this, he turned to Sir Lancelot and said, "You are the best knight in the world. This sword should hang by your side."

"I cannot take this sword. I'm not good enough to carry it. Let us wait for the knight who will find the Holy Grail, for he surely will be the best knight in all the world."

"Well, nephew," said King Arthur, turning to Gawain, "if Sir Lancelot will not pull out this sword, you surely will be able to."

"I shall not be able to take it," replied Sir Gawain, with a shake of his head.

"Try! I command you!" said King Arthur.

Sir Gawain took the sword hilt and pulled, but the sword would not move.

"Gawain," said Lancelot, "you will regret that you ever tried to move this sword. Great harm will come to you because you tried when you were not the right man."

"I could not go against a command of the king," replied Sir Gawain.

"Sir Percival!" called out King Arthur. "Come, take hold of this sword and try to pull it from the stone that holds it!"

Sir Percival tried, in order to keep Gawain company, but he could not move the sword either.

"I think we have had adventure enough," Sir Kay interrupted before Sir Lancelot could be cross with Sir Percival. "Let's go back to the hall and begin our feast."

More wonders were to occur, for as they started to eat all the doors and windows in the hall suddenly shut, with no man's hand to close them, and the hall became dark. In the darkness an old man appeared in their midst. With him was a young knight with a red cross on his tunic, who carried no shield or sword, although a scabbard hung empty at his side. No one saw them enter the hall.

The old man spoke to King Arthur, "My lord, I bring you a young knight, called Sir Galahad. He received his knighthood earlier today from Sir Lancelot."

"You are both welcome to my court," said King Arthur.

The old man led the young man to The Seat of Danger, between Sir

Lancelot and Sir Percival and removed the silken cloth. There they all saw letters of gold which read:

THIS IS THE SEAT OF GALAHAD THE HIGH PRINCE.

"Here is your place at the Round Table, Sir Galahad," he said, and he departed from the hall.

Sir Lancelot looked at his son who was sitting next to him, and he was full of joy and happiness. Many in the hall, seeing them sit side by side saw the likeness and the word spread quickly round the table that Galahad was Sir Lancelot's son.

King Arthur went over and looked at the name in Sir Galahad's place. "I have something strange and wonderful to show you," he said to the young man. "Come with me!"

He led Galahad to the river, where he pointed out the sword still standing in the slab of stone. "The best knights in my court have tried to pull that sword from the stone, but have failed."

"This is no wonder to me," replied Sir Galahad, "for this adventure is mine!" So saying, he took hold of the sword and pulled it gently. It slid with ease from the stone, and Galahad placed it in his scabbard.

The king was greatly moved to see this. "Sir Galahad, you are going to bring great honour to the Knights of the Round Table," he said. "Allow me to present you with a shield."

Sir Galahad shook his head. "I need no shield from you my lord. Just as I have found the sword that was meant for me, so I shall find a shield."

King Arthur announced to the assembled company, "Today, for the first time since the Round Table came to Camelot, every seat has been filled. To celebrate we will have a great tournament followed by another feast tomorrow."

The jousting field was crowded early the next morning. Many of the ladies, with Queen Guinevere, came to watch the tournament from a tower. Knights and horses were all excited, and squires and pages ran to and fro with swords and spears. King Arthur was anxious to see how well Sir Galahad jousted, and there were many ready to challenge him to a fight. Galahad, dressed in red armour,

and with his new sword to hand, willingly took the spear that he was offered. He still carried no shield.

One after the other different knights broke their spears against Sir Galahad, who defeated them all. Only Sir Lancelot and Sir Percival did not fight with him. Then the king invited Galahad to remove his helmet under the queen's tower, so she could see his face.

"I never saw any son so like his father in all my life. It is no surprise to me that he excels so in the tournament," the queen said.

That evening, as all the knights sat at the Round Table, the sky darkened and a great clap of thunder almost deafened them. Then a brilliant beam of light shone through the hall, casting a brightness on all those it touched. Each knight looked on his fellow knights and saw qualities of goodness in his companions that he had not seen before. And while the light shone, each man found he could not speak.

Now the Holy Grail entered on the beam of light and travelled round the hall. It was covered with a white cloth, and was held high but no man could see whose hand held it. Only when it disappeared and the bright light faded, could the knights speak once more.

King Arthur was the first. "We should thank God that we have seen this marvellous sight."

Now Gawain called out, "It is a sign that we should seek the Holy Grail. Who will go on this quest?"

At once many voices cried out, "I will, I will," until the whole hall was in clamour, and the king held up his hand for silence. He looked with pride and love at the men who sat at The Round Table with him and spoke with a voice that rang with emotion.

"This feast of Whitsun has brought great happiness and joy, for Sir Galahad has taken his place in the Seat of Danger. We have also seen the Holy Grail. If you go on this quest, which will be the hardest quest of all, many of you will never return, so it is a day of great sadness too. Merlin spoke of this time when the last seat at the Round Table would be taken by the Perfect Knight. When this happened he said that the end of the fellowship of the Round Table would be near. Now I see the truth in Merlin's words."

17

THE QUEST OF THE HOLY GRAIL

The Knights of the Round Table, in answer to Gawain's challenge, rode out from Camelot on a quest for the Holy Grail. King Arthur and Queen Guinevere wept as they bade them farewell.

Sir Gawain, was one of the first to depart, and behind him rode his brothers, Sir Gareth, Sir Agravaine and Sir Gaheris. Sir Galahad, his young face shining with excitement, was near the front of the long line of knights. Sir Ector de Maris and Sir Lionel rode out together, followed by Sir Lancelot and Sir Percival and Sir Bedivere. Sir Tor rode with Sir Griflet, and Sir Uwain rode beside King Bagdemagus. Knights in red armour, knights in black armour, knights with red, blue and green pennants set out through the gates of Camelot.

No one knew which way to go or what adventures he might encounter in his efforts to find the Holy Grail, so each knight chose the direction he thought best. As the sound of their horses' hooves faded and the dust settled, an empty silence hung over Camelot.

* * *

Sir Galahad set out on the quest of the Holy Grail with the sword he had pulled from the slab of marble in the river but he still carried no shield. On the fourth day, as he approached an abbey, some monks came out to greet him, and made him welcome in their guest chamber. There, to his delight, he found two other Knights of the Round Table, King Bagdemagus and Sir Uwain. "What brings you here?" he asked them.

"We hear there is a shield in this abbey which no man may carry

140

without receiving a grievous wound, unless he is the knight for whom the shield is waiting. Tomorrow I am going to try my luck," said King Bagdemagus.

"Only the best knight in the world may carry this shield," advised a monk.

"Well, I am not the best knight, but I intend to see how I fare," declared King Bagdemagus.

The next day he rode out from the abbey with a squire and carried the white shield with a red cross on it that the monks had taken from behind the altar in the abbey church. He had not gone far before he came to a place where the hermit Nanciens lived. A knight in shining white armour rode out from behind the hermit's hut, and challenged him. They fought for only a short while before King Bagdemagus fell heavily to the ground with a severe wound in his shoulder.

The knight in white armour dismounted and took the shield from King Bagdemagus, and gave it to the squire. "Take this back to the abbey and present it to Sir Galahad. He is the only knight worthy of carrying this shield."

Sir Galahad received the shield, and rode back with the squire to the knight in white armour. "My name is Sir Galahad. Please tell me where the shield comes from and why I should be the one to carry it."

"That shield was brought to this land by Joseph of Arimathea. The red cross is made with his blood. It has been waiting for you for hundreds of years, Sir Galahad, for you are the true descendant of this most holy man, and you are the Perfect Knight."

Now the squire who had ridden with Galahad knelt before him and asked to be made a knight, so he could ride with him on the quest of the Holy Grail. He felt sure he had more chance of success on the quest if he stayed close to Galahad. "My name is Melias de Lile, I am son of the King of Denmark," he said.

Sir Galahad made Melias a knight and they rode on together. But when they had a choice of ways they parted. After two days, Sir Melias came to a clearing in a wood where a table was laid with food and a golden crown was set on the table. Sir Melias, who was not hungry, took up the crown to examine it. Before he knew what was happening, a huge knight rode out of the trees and attacked him. Sir Melias was severely wounded, and would have died if Sir Galahad had not come by another path and defeated Sir Melias' opponent. He then took Melias to an abbey where a hermit with the gift of healing promised to restore the young man to health.

Sir Galahad was always the victor in any contest as he rode across the land in search of the Holy Grail. He was put to many tests of bravery and honesty, but each time he did the right thing and rode on further in his quest.

On one occasion he defeated both Sir Lancelot and Sir Percival in combat. Neither knew whom they fought, because Sir Galahad had his helmet down and they did not recognise the white shield with the red cross.

As Sir Galahad rode away, a girl came from a hermit's hut and called out, "God go with you, for you are the best knight in the world." Lancelot immediately realised that he had just fought against his own son, and rode after him. But Galahad, who wanted to seek the Holy Grail alone, spurred on his horse and galloped even faster until he had shaken Sir Lancelot off his trail.

Sir Lancelot, knowing he was unworthy of the highest honour of the Holy Grail, went to a chapel where he repented of all things he had done in his life which made it impossible for him to continue with the quest. Nanciens, the hermit, listened to him and instructed him on the virtues required by the knights on the quest of the Holy Grail.

* * *

Sir Percival, after he had been defeated by Sir Galahad, rode off in a different direction from Sir Lancelot, and came to a hermit's hut where he met a holy lady who told him she was his aunt. She explained how Sir Galahad had acquired the holy shield of Joseph of Arimathea, and encouraged Percival to ride on, seeking to do good and brave deeds. "In time," she told him, "you will get near to the Holy Grail, and if you resist evil temptations you will find your heart's desire, which is, I think, the lady Blanchefleur."

142

Encouraged, Sir Percival rode out again, no longer angry with Sir Galahad for defeating him in combat, but anxious to join with him if he could in the quest. As he rode along a narrow valley he met twenty armed men who challenged him and demanded his name.

"I am Sir Percival from the court of King Arthur!" he called back.

When they heard this they cried out, "Attack! Attack! We are bound to kill all those from King Arthur's court."

Percival fought bravely, and killed the first man to strike him, and his horse, but then he was set on by seven men at the same time. He was soon knocked onto the ground and his horse was killed. He would have died if a knight carrying a white shield with a red cross had not ridden up at that moment and set about Percival's enemies, striking to right and left, first with his spear and then, when that was shattered, with his sword. When all lay dead he rode off.

Sir Percival, realising that the man who had just saved him was Sir Galahad called out for him to wait, and then started to run after him. Sir Galahad did not hear, and was soon far away, leaving Sir Percival struggling through the forest on foot.

In the evening, as he sat dispirited and exhausted, a lady approached leading the finest black horse Percival had ever seen. "Do you need a horse, Sir Percival?" she asked. "Why don't you take this one for your journey?"

Percival could not believe his good fortune, and leapt on the horse. He was astonished by its speed. It seemed almost to fly, and in one hour he covered as much ground as he would normally expect to travel in four days. But it galloped so fast that he could not stop it. To his horror, it led him right up to a huge roaring torrent of water and was on the point of plunging in. Percival knew he could not live in such a river. It suddenly crossed his mind that he might be riding the devil's horse, and he made the sign of a cross. Instantly, the horse pulled up, snorting and neighing, and as Percival landed on the ground the horse disappeared.

Towards evening the next day, Percival found himself beside the sea, in a small bay. A beautiful maiden came to him and talked to him of Sir Galahad and the quest they were both on. She brought him delicious food, and when he admired her, she invited him to kiss her and be true only to her for the rest of his life. He was leaning forward to kiss her, when he remembered Blanchefleur. As he hesitated, he made a sign of the cross. The maiden shrieked in rage and disappeared in a great tearing wind, leaving Percival alone by the edge of the water.

"I am being tempted, as my aunt told me I would be," said Sir Percival, sadly, as he shivered with cold on the sea shore, and wondered how he would ever find Sir Galahad.

As dawn broke, he saw a ship had sailed into the bay. A lady on the ship called out to him, "Come, Percival. This ship will take you nearer to the Holy Grail. Soon Sir Galahad will join us on it, and Sir Bors, who will be witness of all you and Sir Galahad do."

Cautious in case this might be another trap, Sir Percival asked, "Who are you and how do you know my name?"

"I am your sister, although we have never met. I have been sent by the hermit Nanciens, to tell you that you have overcome the temptations. Put on your armour and come on to the ship."

And Percival went on to the ship, full of joy that he was still on the quest of the Holy Grail.

* * *

Sir Bors was a quiet and gentle knight, not known for any great and marvellous acts of bravery. He was surprised, therefore, when he came to a hermit's hut that he was called in. "Welcome, Sir Bors. My name is Nanciens. Come and learn from me how you will play your part in the quest for the Holy Grail," said the old man.

In the days that followed Sir Bors learnt that he would be sent trials and tests, but he must be good and honourable and must not take the easy way. "You will go with Sir Galahad and Sir Percival to the place where the Holy Grail is," advised the holy man, "and then your task will be to return to Camelot and tell King Arthur what you have seen, for neither Sir Galahad nor Sir Percival will return. You are to be the witness."

For some days after Sir Bors left the hermit's hut he did not find any special adventures. Then, as he was riding along he heard a terrible groaning, and he turned to see two armed robbers leading a horse with man bound and wounded lying across it. He saw to his horror that the wounded man was his brother Lionel. He was just pulling out his sword, for he knew he must rescue his brother before he came to more harm, when he heard a woman's voice calling from the other direction, "Help! Help me!" A lady whom he had never seen before was being attacked by armed robbers.

Sir Bors knew it was his duty to help a lady in trouble, and yet he longed to save his brother. Putting duty first he quickly attacked the robbers, and rescued the lady, and would have then turned to help his brother Lionel, but she begged him to escort her to her castle and there stay and protect her. Seeing no choice he went with the lady.

When he was in her castle she offered him many temptations, all of which he refused. Finally she took him up on top of a high tower where twenty maidens stood. "Please grant the lady of the castle what she wants, or she will force all of us to jump from these high walls, and we will most certainly die. If this happens, you will be responsible for our deaths." Sir Bors made the sign of the cross while he asked God's guidance in this choice. Instantly the castle and all the ladies were gone in a rushing wind, and Sir Bors found himself standing on a bare hillside.

Early the next morning, as he was walking towards the nearest castle where he hoped he might get a horse, he found himself face to face with his brother Lionel, who sat astride his horse. Sir Bors thought that when he had seen his brother as a prisoner of armed robbers the day before it must have been a bad dream, and so he greeted his brother with delight. But Sir Lionel said, "So, you are the brother who left me to my fate yesterday. Turn away from me, for I no longer consider you a brother of mine."

Sir Bors begged forgiveness, but Sir Lionel would have none of it. "If you will not ride away, you must fight me," shouted Sir Lionel, still angry.

Sir Bors did not know what to do, for brother should never fight brother. In addition, Sir Lionel was older than him, and Sir Bors knew his duty was always to respect him. He knelt on the ground as he wondered what to do, and Sir Lionel, with a roar of rage, unsheathed his sword and attacked him.

Sir Bors would have been dead in minutes if Nanciens, the hermit, had not rushed upon the scene and ordered Sir Lionel to stop. "If you kill your brother now, you will bring great harm to the kingdom. He has a part to play in the quest of the Holy Grail."

Nanciens led them both to an abbey where Sir Bors rested for some days, and Sir Lionel stayed for a year. There he talked of many things to the wise monks, and asked their forgiveness for all that he had done wrong in his life.

Sir Bors rode away from the abbey, and he came in a few days to the sea, where he found the ship with Percival awaiting him.

"Welcome," he cried, "now we only lack Sir Galahad. When he comes we will sail to the waste lands where we will find the castle of Carbonek. It is in this place that we will find the Holy Grail."

18

THE KNIGHT OF THE HOLY GRAIL

As the Knights of the Round Table sought the Holy Grail, they had different adventures. Many died and some received terrible wounds, but those who returned alive to Camelot had marvellous tales to tell, although none had found the Holy Grail.

Sir Galahad had many adventures, but he always rode on, determined, if he could, to find the Holy Grail. In time he arrived at the coast, where he saw the ship where Sir Percival and Sir Bors waited for him.

"Greetings, Galahad," they called out. "We hoped you would be here before too long."

As they sailed towards the waste lands, Sir Percival and Sir Bors explained to Galahad many of the things that Nanciens, the hermit, had told them. In addition they all had their own adventures to tell to each other. Eventually the ship came to a land so desolate and bare that they knew they must be nearly at the castle of Carbonek.

"All living things on this land were destroyed when King Pelles was wounded so many years ago," Sir Bors told them. "Only when one of us holds the Holy Grail will the land come back to life."

Now Sir Percival remembered being here before, and said he would lead the way. They left the ship and rode on horses that were waiting for them until they came to a castle with old and cracked walls. As they mounted the steps at the entrance, they found themselves full of wonder that anyone could live there.

Inside, at one end of the hall a fire was burning. Near the fire, for he shivered with cold even in the heat of summer, King Pelles lay on his couch. The wound he had received so many years before had never healed and he could not walk. Galahad, Percival and Bors bowed their heads as they greeted him. With great dignity King Pelles bade them welcome.

To Sir Galahad he said, "I am your grandfather, King Pelles. Many years have I lain here sick and waiting for you."

He brought out from behind his couch a sword that was broken in three pieces. "I must ask each of you if you can mend it," he said.

First Sir Bors tried, but he could not make the pieces fit, then Sir Percival attempted it. In his hands they nearly came together, but it was not a perfect fit. Only when Sir Galahad held all three pieces did the sword become whole once more.

"Now I know which of you is the Grail Knight," King Pelles said.

Even as he spoke, a fearful darkness filled the room and a strong cold wind blew through it. Then a brilliant beam of light shone in the room, casting light on a strange procession. Three maidens, each clothed in white walked through the hall, and each bore a precious object before her. The first maiden held a cup of silver from which shone a strong glowing light. The second maiden bore high in the air a candlestick with seven burning candles. The third maiden carried a spear from which drops of blood hung but never fell to the floor.

"What do all these things mean?" Galahad whispered to the old man.

"It is good that you have asked this question. If Percival had asked it when he was here before I would have been cured and my lands would no longer be desolate and dead. Follow the maiden and you will find out what it all means," King Pelles said.

The three men found themselves following behind the procession. Walking slowly and following the light from the cup and from the candles, they went through a door and along a narrow passage. Here the maidens turned and walked into the chapel, followed by Galahad, Percival and Bors.

Now moving as in a dream, Galahad went up to the altar, where Nanciens stood. Raising his right hand, the old hermit said, "Now the Maimed King can be made well. The spear which you see is the same spear which pierced the side of Jesus when he hung upon the cross. Take it to King Pelles, and hold it to his wounds."

Galahad took the spear to where his wounded grandfather lay and held it to his side. Even while he held it, the damaged flesh became whole and King Pelles found he could stand beside his couch.

Now Galahad returned to the chapel, where he moved to the altar and took the cup from Nanciens.

"For too many years I have been guardian of this cup, brought to this land by Joseph of Arimathea. I am happy to hand over its guardianship to you."

Before their eyes the old man, who had been so good to them all, seemed to shrink and wither, and he fell senseless on the ground. Sir Bors was the first to reach him, and found he was dead.

As Sir Galahad held the cup in his hands, Sir Percival looked at the maiden who had been carrying it, and found he was gazing at Blanchefleur.

"I have sought you high and low," he told her, "and have given my heart to no other lady since we parted. How happy I am to see you again."

After they had all thanked God in the chapel for all the miraculous happenings of that day, they gathered in King Pelles' hall for a feast. Birdsong drowned their talk, and when they looked out they saw trees bursting into leaf and green grass springing from dry desolate earth. All around them were signs of life and new growth.

King Pelles told them of Sir Lancelot's visit to the Castle of Carbonek, and how he had been unable to come into the chapel of the Holy Grail. "He lay unconscious in this hall for twenty-four days, and we feared he was dead. In spite of being the best knight in all the world for so long, neither he nor Gawain could achieve what you have achieved, Galahad."

* * *

Two years after the start of the Quest of the Holy Grail Sir Bors rode into Camelot just before the Whitsun feast. When Sir Lancelot and Sir Gawain saw him approach they called King Arthur, for they knew that Sir Bors had been with Sir Galahad and Sir Percival on the quest.

Many knights and ladies crowded round, full of questions. Sir Bors

told them as much as he was able. He described to them the night when Sir Galahad had held the spear to King Pelles' side and his wound had been healed. He talked of how the land round the castle of Carbonek had grown green and lush once more. He told them of the death of Nanciens, the old hermit and keeper of the Grail.

"Tell us what happened to Percival?" King Arthur asked.

"Percival has met his beloved Blanchefleur," Sir Bors told them. "They were married by Galahad, who became a priest, and Percival is now living with her in Carbonek."

"And King Pelles?" someone asked, before Lancelot could ask news of Galahad.

"King Pelles died. He lived to enjoy freedom from pain for only a short time. He said he was happy to die, for he had been trying to stay alive only until his country was freed from the curse that made all vegetation die. The land grows green again, and he died a happy man."

"And Galahad?" asked Sir Lancelot.

Sir Bors was silent for a few moments, then he looked at Sir Lancelot with sorrow in his eyes. "He is dead too. I stayed to bury him near Nanciens and King Pelles."

"Why should Galahad, the Perfect Knight die so young?" one of the ladies asked.

"I think," said Sir Bors, "it was because he alone had led a blameless and a faultless life. It was for this reason he was able to become the Grail Knight. But no man can continue to live without faults, and so it was better he died young than lived to join the rest of us in our mistakes and wrong doings. He asked me to say, Sir Lancelot, that he prayed for you, for we knew you had been to Carbonek, but had been unable to achieve the quest of the Holy Grail."

King Arthur said, "you bring us happy news and sad. We have other sadness around us, for nearly half the Knights of the Round Table have died in the past two years while they sought the Holy Grail. Each one, it seems, was only able to prove his own imperfections. We thank you, Sir Bors, for going to Carbonek and bringing us back the story of Sir Galahad, the Knight of the Grail. For all the sadness of the tale, it has brought great honour to Camelot."

* * *

No one at Camelot asked, "What happened to the Holy Grail?" If they had, Sir Bors would probably not have known the answer. After Galahad's death, it disappeared, and the stories that surrounded it have ceased. But somewhere, in a quiet place, where a castle once stood, and where holy men came, a precious cup lies hidden and forgotten.

One day it may be found again.

19

THE END OF THE ROUND TABLE

King Arthur surveyed his Round Table and was sad. Only seventy knights had returned from the Quest of the Holy Grail, and many seats remained empty at the table. No more, it seemed, did young men ride in to Camelot and find their names written in gold by the places that awaited them. Gawain and Lancelot, two of his oldest friends were sadly changed since they had returned from the quest, and there was less laughter and friendship among all the knights. He himself felt old and tired.

Ugly rumours persisted, too, that made Arthur uneasy. How much longer could he ignore the gossip that told him that Lancelot and Guinevere were seeing each other secretly? He thought of Merlin, his old friend and adviser who had seen harm to the fellowship of the Round Table in his marriage to Guinevere. Yet his own love for Guinevere was so great that he could not imagine anything changing it, not even Lancelot's love for her.

Arthur and Guinevere had no children, but Arthur had a son, Mordred, born before he married Guinevere, and now his thoughts turned to him. He summoned Mordred to Camelot, and he and Guinevere adopted him.

Sometimes, Arthur saw flashes of ambition and restlessness in Mordred. His mother, Morgause, had always been ambitious for Mordred. Was he impatient to be king now? If so, what should he do, for he, Arthur, was not ready to give up his kingship yet. Should he give Mordred more responsibility or send him away from Camelot?

Many others in Camelot seemed to be dissatisfied too. Queen Guinevere longed to see more of Lancelot, and fretted whenever he was away. Lancelot, who for many years, had fought against his violent passion for the queen, rode out of Camelot as often as possible, as he used to when he was a young man, to avoid seeing the queen as much as they both desired. Many of the younger knights were jealous of the favours King Arthur showed to Mordred. All round Camelot groups of men gathered and muttered, and made plots to belittle one knight or another. Mordred, too, was unhappy because he feared King Arthur was no longer interested in keeping his old enemies under control.

Agravaine, one of Gawain's younger brothers, who was always ready to pick a quarrel, and was jealous of Lancelot, took Mordred on one side, and made a plan. "The king shows too many favours to Lancelot. Let's set a trap and prove once and for all that he visits the queen's rooms at night. Then the king will banish him from Camelot, and there will be more favours for us."

Mordred did not like the plan, but he agreed that life at Camelot might be easier without Lancelot. So, that night a message came to Lancelot, inviting him to visit the queen. Lancelot, who believed the message came from Guinevere, went along to her rooms. Since it was evening, he went, unarmed. He had not been with Guinevere for more than a few minutes when a dreadful banging and knocking started on the door.

"Open up! Open up!" a voice called. "We know you are with the queen. Open the door, you traitor!"

Lancelot turned to the queen. "Do you have any arms here?"

"No! And it would be unwise to fight. I can hear many voices out there! What are we to do?"

Lancelot opened the door a crack. Immediately Colgrevance, the man nearest to the door, pushed through. In one swift movement Lancelot shut the door before any one else could follow, and dealt Colgrevance a tremendous blow. Even before he had fallen to the floor Lancelot had seized his sword.

"Stop! Lancelot! You will be killed!" Guinevere called out, but it was too late. Lancelot was out in the passage, attacking the men who had set a trap for him. There were eleven, and using the confined space to his advantage, Lancelot killed ten of them. The last man,

Mordred, he only wounded, before he rushed from Camelot.

The palace was in uproar. The queen's ladies came to soothe her, while word went quickly to Arthur that eleven knights were dead in the palace, killed by Lancelot. Sir Mordred was wounded and Sir Lancelot, who had been found in the queen's rooms had fled from Camelot.

"What am I to do?" Arthur cried in anguish. Then, almost smiling in the midst of his horror he said, "Lancelot has killed eleven armed men single handed? He always has been a wonderful knight!"

"The queen must be burnt at the stake, for that is the punishment for an unfaithful queen," Sir Kay reminded him. "And Lancelot should be killed too, or banished.

All night King Arthur wrestled with the problem of what he should do. He knew that Sir Kay was right and Guinevere his beloved wife should be tied to the stake and burnt.

At dawn he called Gawain to him. "You have heard of this dreadful night's happenings? You know your brother Agravaine is dead?" he asked. "I want you to arrange for Guinevere to be burnt at the stake. I can't bring myself to arrange it myself."

"Uncle, you cannot do this," exclaimed Gawain. "You will destroy everything the Round Table has stood for if you put Guinevere to death."

"You could say that Lancelot has already done that," Arthur said.

"Well, I will not make matters worse," replied Gawain. "I refuse to have anything to do with Guinevere's death."

King Arthur now called Gawain's brothers, Gareth and Gaheris to him, and told them to arrange for Guinevere to be burnt at the stake. He instructed them to escort her there. They did not dare, like Gawain, to refuse the king altogether, but Gareth, who was known for his gentleness said, "We will do this, if we must, although it will be the saddest day of our lives. But we cannot go as armed knights. We will escort the queen unarmed."

By midday a huge fire had been built and the stake to which Guinevere was to be tied as she burnt, was in place. Slowly, and with great sadness Guinevere walked towards the stake, with Gareth on one side and Gaheris on the other. She did not dare look back for a final glimpse of her home and of King Arthur. The brothers bowed their heads as they walked with her.

In a flurry of dust and a thunder of hooves a horseman swept up to the small group. Before anyone could see what was happening, the rider thrust his sword at each of the men with Guinevere, and they fell sprawling on the ground. Then Guinevere was lifted on to the horseman's saddle and she was taken away, at high speed, into the forest.

"It was Sir Lancelot!" the cry went up. "Sir Lancelot has snatched away the queen."

Gawain ran forward and knelt by his brothers. Gareth and Gaheris were both dead. "He has killed them! He has killed them!" he kept repeating in a strange, strangled voice. "Lancelot must die for this. Gareth loved him more than any man. Lancelot has killed Gareth."

"Come, Gawain," King Arthur said, "it was I who asked them to go with Guinevere. I am sure Lancelot did not look to see whom he killed."

"But he has killed my brothers. Lancelot must die."

Everyone was in a state of shock, and while Gawain was calling for Lancelot's death, Arthur did not know whether to weep or laugh – for he felt unashamed joy that Guinevere was still alive.

Lancelot rode as fast as he could with Guinevere and a group of his friends to one of his castles called Joyous Gard. There he quickly prepared for a siege, for he knew Arthur would send an armed force to bring back Guinevere. For nearly three months Arthur's army camped outside Joyous Gard. The walls were too strong for them to attack it, so their only hope was that Lancelot and all those in the castle would starve or give themselves up. Each day Gawain rode up and called out to Lancelot, challenging him to fight him and to let the queen return to Camelot. Day after day Lancelot refused the taunts and stayed inside the castle. At last his patience broke, and one day he leant over the battlements and called out, "You will never take this castle. You are wasting your time."

"Come out and fight me in single combat, instead of staying in there like a coward," King Arthur called back.

"I could never fight you in single combat. You are the high king,

and the finest king in all the world. Also, you gave me my knighthood. How could I fight you?"

"But you have made yourself my enemy by taking Guinevere away!"

"If you pardon Guinevere, I will leave this land and never more be seen in Camelot or in your kingdom," Lancelot proposed.

The king nearly agreed, but again Gawain shouted, "Lancelot must die. I will kill him myself if no one else will."

The next day, Lancelot, with a group of armed men from the castle, made a surprise attack on the king's camp. In the fighting Gawain slew Sir Lionel as he tried to get close to Lancelot, and Sir Bors, who fought with Lancelot, knocked the king from his horse. He held his sword to King Arthur's throat, and said, "Shall I slay him?"

"Never!" cried Lancelot. "King Arthur shall never die at my hand or the hand of one of my friends." And he helped the king to his feet.

Now King Arthur made peace with Lancelot and pardoned Guinevere. She was led out of Joyous Gard and returned to Camelot with the king. But Arthur's heart was sad, for his worst fears had been realised. Knight of the Round Table had slain Knight of the Round Table. The fellowship he had created of all the finest knights in the land was destroyed.

Gawain was furious, and would not agree that the peace extended to him. He returned to Camelot still swearing vengeance on Lancelot for killing his brothers. But Lancelot, true to his word, went to live in France with many of his friends and followers.

For some while, life at Camelot returned to normal, except that the atmosphere was even more uncomfortable than before, and everyone was very nervous. King Arthur hoped that things would get better, although he could not see how this could happen. Jealousies worsened, tempers frayed, and Gawain, who missed his brothers most terribly, fretted and fumed, urging Arthur to make war on Lancelot again.

At last Arthur, worn down by Gawain's arguments, agreed. He hoped that if the knights who still remained loyal to him fought together, it might unite them. So Arthur led an expedition of fighting men to France.

Since it seemed that Mordred was at the centre of much of the unrest among the knights, Arthur decided it would be best if Mordred stayed at Camelot. He arranged for Mordred to look after the kingdom and to take care of Guinevere.

In France, many months went by while Arthur and Gawain besieged Lancelot's castle. At last Lancelot agreed to fight Gawain in single combat. For so many years these two had been the finest knights in the fellowship of the Round Table, and been good friends. They had not fought each other since they were young men, and then only in a friendly tournament. Neither had ever been beaten by another knight, except by Sir Galahad. Now they fought in deadly earnest. Three times they fought and three times Lancelot grievously wounded Gawain. Yet still Gawain would not give up, shouting to anyone who would listen, "As long as I have breath left in my body, I swear to kill Lancelot. He slew my brothers." It seemed to many that Gawain was like a madman.

Arthur wondered, as the weeks and months went by, why no letters came from England. Some said there had been bad storms, others made different excuses for letters not to arrive. Then, one evening, a messenger rode in to Arthur's camp. He was so exhausted he could hardly speak for he had ridden day and night. To Arthur's surprise, the messenger was one of Guinevere's servants. "What is it? Is the queen all right? Why have you come?" Arthur asked urgently.

"My lord, I have a letter from the queen. It was difficult to get through Mordred's spies at the ports, or I would have been here many days ago."

With shaking hands, Arthur took the letter, and read:

"My lord Arthur,
If you are alive, I beg you to come quickly. Mordred tells me he has heard news of your death, but no messenger has come to tell us this is true. Mordred has made treaties with some of your enemies which you gave him no rights to do. He plans to be crowned king, and he demands that I should marry him and be his queen. I pretended to agree in order not to arouse his

suspicions, and have now taken refuge in an abbey. His men watch all the ports to stop news of his activities from reaching you. Please come back here and bring all the fighting men you can, for you may have to do battle with Mordred to regain your kingdom.

Guinevere."

Arthur immediately called all the knights who were with him to his tent, and read the letter aloud.

"Do any of you know about this treachery?"

They shook their heads. He heard someone muttering, "But Mordred was always ambitious."

"We must ride to the coast immediately, and cross the sea to England as soon as possible." Gawain spoke from the couch on which he lay most days now, as the wound he had received from Lancelot was still not healed. "We must send messengers ahead to organise the boats."

With all haste, Arthur's supporters left their camp near Lancelot's castle and rode northwards to the coast. They boarded a fleet of boats to sail to England, and arrived at Dover. But news of their coming travelled ahead of them, and Mordred's forces were waiting on the beach as they tried to land.

Many of Arthur's supporters were killed even before they set foot on land. But Arthur fought back, and within two hours the enemy had fled over the cliffs, leaving Arthur and Bedivere, his close friend, to count the dead and arrange for their burial.

"What a homecoming!" Arthur said in a shaken voice.

Word came that Sir Gawain wished to speak to the king as soon as possible. Arthur found his old friend was dying, and knelt close to him. "This is all my fault," Gawain said. "If I had not urged you to fight Lancelot, all this would never have happened. Now the only hope of saving your kingdom is to send for Lancelot. Will you help me write a letter to him, for I am very weak?"

Gawain's letter to Lancelot said,

"Sir Lancelot,

You must consider yourself the victor in our quarrel. The wound you gave me has been opened up again in the fighting today, and I will die before tomorrow's daybreak. Make no mistake I am dying because of the wound you gave me, so consider yourself the victor. Our quarrel was not of Arthur's making. He constantly urged me to make peace with you. He now desperately needs your help, so come with all the men you can bring to fight with him against Mordred, who has seized the throne.

Farewell, great knight, for if you answer this call and come you will find me in my grave. Only now that I am dying can I see how a madness has been driving me to hate you, but this madness has now gone, and I think of you as you always were, as my friend. Come and save Arthur's kingdom if you can.

Gawain."

As Gawain finished the letter his hand grew limp. Arthur held water to his lips, but he could not drink. Within the hour Sir Gawain was dead.

Arthur knelt by his friend's body for many hours, weeping and grieving for the death of this fine knight and good old friend.

"We must bury Sir Gawain with all the honour due to such a fine knight," he said, "and then we must ride with all haste to the west, where many loyal supporters will rally to my royal flag. I cannot believe that Mordred will have many followers when the people hear that I have returned. Let Mordred challenge my army if he chooses. We'll drive Mordred the Usurper from our land, rescue the queen and return to Camelot."

King Arthur raised his sword Excalibur above his head.

His companions smiled to see the bravado of their king return. "Down with Mordred the Traitor!" they all cried.

And so they rode west to prepare for the last battle.

20

THE LAST BATTLE

The air was hot and close and storm clouds threatened as King Arthur rode to the west. Mordred, his son, had seized the throne and attacked him when he arrived back in England, and now Arthur was following Mordred's army and seeking more support for himself. Sir Bedivere and Sir Lucan, two of Arthur's oldest friends rode with him. But so many of the Knights of the Round Table were now dead, or living in France near Sir Lancelot with whom they had sided against King Arthur and Sir Gawain that Arthur sensed a great emptiness and desolation as he rode. He had just buried his favourite nephew, Gawain, and this death added immeasurably to his deep sense of loss.

King Arthur's mind turned to the great and glorious days when still a boy he had pulled his sword from the stone, and been proclaimed king; he remembered when he had won his first battle against rival kings; he thought of Guinevere constantly, and how she had come to Camelot as his queen. On their wedding day he had founded the fellowship of the Knights of the Round Table. It seemed then that only good could come from all he did. But now knight was turned against knight, and evil in the shape of his own son was riding across the land, destroying everything that he, Arthur, had lived and worked for.

Arthur's plan was to organise a strong army and confront Mordred. Many had already come out and joined him. If he had to fight he would, but he hoped that a sufficient show of strength would bring an end to Mordred's treachery. Then he could fetch Guinevere from London where she was sheltering, and bring her once more to Camelot. To start all over again would be hard, but he could try to build a new fellowship of the Round Table, and establish trust once more amongst a new generation of knights.

Arthur, and his growing army paused for a few days at Camlann, a place where sea and marsh, river and plain all came together. He was discussing his plans with Bedivere and Lucan when a messenger rode in. "My lord, Sir Mordred has amassed a large army. Many of his fighting men come from the east of England and a great many of those who support Lancelot have joined him, too. He is no more than a day away. He will be here tomorrow."

"Then we must prepare for battle," King Arthur decided. "My men are loyal and will fight well."

King Arthur slept badly that night. It was hot and sticky in his tent, and the thunder which always threatened, never seemed to come. While he tossed restlessly, Arthur had a strange and horrible nightmare. He saw himself sitting in all his finest clothes in a huge chair or throne, which was on a platform. The platform was attached to an enormous wheel, and as he looked down from a great height he saw a pit below him full of writhing monsters and serpents. Even as he looked, the wheel began to turn, and Arthur found himself being hurled off his chair into this pit, where he was torn apart, limb from limb, by these beasts.

"Help!" he cried out in his sleep. "Help! Help!"

Men rushed to wake him. As he lay there, relief flooded in that he had only been dreaming.

Now he dozed off again, and had another strange dream or vision. His old friend Gawain came to him as though he were still alive and said, "Don't fight this battle tomorrow, Arthur. If you do, you and Mordred will both die and everything you have fought for throughout your life will be lost. Hold peace talks with Mordred, offer him some position. Whatever you agree to need not be for long, because in a month's time Lancelot will join you with his army. Mordred can never win against you and Lancelot when you are united once more. . ." The dream faded, Gawain disappeared and Arthur awoke.

Arthur thought about the advice his dead friend had given him in his dream and called Sir Bedivere and Sir Lucan to him. It was agreed that they would both go with two churchmen to Mordred's camp and offer peace terms.

"Offer Mordred whatever you have to, to buy peace," Arthur instructed.

Mordred made many demands. It was finally agreed that he should become ruler of both Cornwall and Kent immediately, and that when Arthur died he was to rule over all Arthur's kingdom. It was also decided that Arthur and Mordred should meet, accompanied by fourteen people from each side, to sign this agreement.

Mordred was deeply suspicious that there was some trick behind this treaty and the plan to meet with King Arthur, so he told his army leaders that if a sword was drawn while they were meeting, this would be a signal that he had been led into a trap. They were to attack immediately. Arthur likewise feared treachery, and instructed his army to attack immediately if they saw the use of any arms.

So Arthur and Mordred met, each with his own companions, on the plain between the two armies. Wine was brought out and they were drinking to peace, when the unexpected happened. An adder, disturbed by the voices and trampling feet, slid through the grass. Its forked tongue shot out and one of the knights felt a sharp bite on his ankle. With a reflex action the knight drew his sword to kill the poisonous snake. As he did so the sun glinted on the naked metal of his drawn sword.

"Attack! Attack! Mordred has been lured into a trap. There is treachery there," the leaders of Mordred's army cried. Similar shouts went up in Arthur's camp. Before anyone could prevent it, both armies had charged towards each other.

The bloodshed that followed was terrible. All day men and horses fell on the battlefield. The cries of the wounded rang out across the plain, and there seemed no escape for anyone. As the sun went down, the evening sky blazed scarlet, throwing an eerie red glow across the tragic plain. The few men who were left alive, were all severely wounded.

King Arthur paused. He saw only Sir Bedivere and Sir Lucan still standing with him, and Sir Lucan was grievously hurt.

"No one remains from their side," gasped Bedivere.

"Wait, I think that is Mordred walking amongst the wounded and dead," said Arthur. "Give me my spear."

"Stay, we are three, he is one. Our side must be the victors of the battle. Kill no more today," urged Sir Lucan.

"No, it is Mordred's greed and anger against me, his father, that has brought ruin on us all. I must end this day by killing him," said Arthur, still fired by all the fighting.

He took his spear and he charged at the lone figure. Mordred turned just as Arthur reached him and received a fateful blow. With a howl of pain Mordred raised his sword and he brought it down on King Arthur's skull.

Sir Bedivere saw that Mordred was dead and the king dying. "Help me, Lucan. We must move Arthur to the water's edge, where we can bathe his wounds." Painfully and slowly both men dragged their wounded king to the shore, where Lucan collapsed, gasped his last breath and lay still. The strain of moving Arthur had been too much for him.

Bedivere knelt between his dead brother and his dying king and wept. Arthur spoke to him with difficulty. "I grieve too for your brother, Bedivere, for he defended me well and helped me when he needed help himself. But my time is running out, too, and I have a promise to fulfil. I need your help. Take my sword, my noble Excalibur, and throw it into the water. Then come and tell me what you see." Arthur had promised many years before that when he had no more use for Excalibur he would return his magic sword to the Lady of the Lake.

Bedivere took Excalibur from Arthur, but as he went the moonlight glinted on the finely wrought blade and the jewelled hilt. "It would be a shame to throw such a sword into the water where it will be lost forever. I could use this sword after Arthur's death," he thought. "Moreover, if he does not die, he will have need of it himself." So Bedivere placed Excalibur behind a boulder and returned to Arthur.

"I have done as you asked," he said.

"And what did you see?" Arthur asked.

"Nothing," replied Bedivere.

Arthur knew that Bedivere had lied to him. "Oh Bedivere, do not fail me at this moment. You must do as I say, and throw Excalibur into the water."

Bedivere returned to the boulder and took the sword. He was just about to throw it in the water as Arthur had commanded, when he looked at it again and held it in his sword hand. "Arthur will never know if I keep it," he thought and he hid the sword again.

"Now Bedivere, tell me what you saw," said Arthur.

"Nothing, my lord, except that the waters lapped and waves grew dark."

"Oh Bedivere, you have been my friend for so long, do not fail me now. Go again, and this time do as I have asked."

Bedivere returned to where he had hidden the sword. This time he threw it with all his might as far into the water as he could. In the silvery light he saw a hand rise out of the water and grasp the sword by the hilt. Three times the hand brandished the sword in the air and then, still holding it, the hand slid back under the water. No ripples remained on the surface. The water was still and smooth. Bedivere went to King Arthur and told him what he had seen.

"Now I have fulfilled my promise, Excalibur will await me, when I come again," said King Arthur. "Look, a ship has arrived to take me away."

Bedivere saw that a barge had drawn close to the shore. "Carry me there, Bedivere," said the king in a whisper. "I fear I have already stayed too long. Each moment I grow weaker and weaker."

Bedivere carried the king across his shoulders to the barge. Three ladies in black clothes were on board. One was the king's sister, Morgan le Fay, and another was Nimue, the Lady of the Lake. The third was the queen of Northingale. All were weeping and grieving as though they already carried a dead man on the barge.

"Alas, brother, the wound in your head is bad. Come and lie here, and we'll heal you if we can," said Morgan le Fay.

"What shall I do, Arthur, alone amongst our enemies?" cried out Bedivere in anguish as he saw the barge move off.

"I go to the Isle of Avalon, where I hope I may be cured. If you hear no more of me, pray for my soul," King Arthur called in a wavering voice as he floated further away.

Bedivere stood alone on the shore for a long time. Clouds covered the moon and darkness surrounded him. Across the water came the sound of women's voices wailing and crying, grieving for a dying king.

* * *

Some days later, as Bedivere wandered without purpose, he came to a hermit's lodging. Beside the small chapel was a newly dug grave. "Who is buried here?" he asked the hermit.

"I don't know the name of the dead man. Many ladies all dressed in black brought a body here two nights ago, and buried it by the light of a hundred tapers."

"This must be the grave of our dear King Arthur," cried Bedivere, and he knelt beside it and prayed for Arthur's soul.

But no one knows where this grave is that Bedivere found, or even if it is the same grave that others saw later, with a headstone which read:

HERE LIES ARTHUR, THE ONCE AND FUTURE KING

* * *

Of all who fought in that last battle, Sir Bedivere was the only one who lived to tell of that dreadful day of bloodshed and death. He sent messengers to Camelot, to London, to Cornwall and to Wales.

When Guinevere heard the terrible news, she retired to the abbey at Amesbury, where she lived as a nun for the rest of her life. Everything she and Arthur had hoped to achieve in Camelot was in ruins, and she wanted to take no more part in the world.

Sir Lancelot received the letter Sir Gawain wrote on his deathbed, and came with a large fighting force to help King Arthur against his rebel son Mordred. The first news he received on landing was that Sir Gawain was dead. Lancelot knelt by the grave of his old friend and rival and wept with sorrow that they had quarrelled so bitterly.

As he rode west Lancelot learnt of the dreadful massacre that had taken place on the field at Camlann. No King Arthur; no court at Camelot; not even Arthur's son, the traitor Mordred, was alive. He heard that Guinevere had gone to the convent at Amesbury and he decided that he too should retire from the world and devote the rest of his life to God.

Some years later, when he heard of Guinevere's death, Lancelot rode to Amesbury and accompanied her body to Glastonbury, where she was buried. When Lancelot died, the monks of Glastonbury buried him in the same tomb as Guinevere.

So, finally, in death, Lancelot and Guinevere were together and at peace. They had loved each so dearly, yet it was their love as much as Mordred's ambition, which destroyed the fellowship of the Knights of the Round Table.

* * *

King Arthur, the legends say, will come again to Britain when he is most needed. He will return with his sword Excalibur, to fight for right, for honour and for truth.

PEOPLE WHO APPEAR IN THE STORIES

The numbers in brackets refer to the stories in which they appear

Abellus: A knight who ran off with a white hound (6)

Accolan: A knight of the Round Table, Lover of Morgan le Fay (8)

Agravaine: A Knight of the Round Table, Arthur's nephew, brother of Gawain and son of King Lot and Queen Morgause (11, 17, 19)

Alardin of the Isles: A knight who is killed by Sir Gawain (6)

Allewes: An evil enchantress (9)

Arthur: High King (All stories)

Bagdemagus: A king and a Knight of the Round Table, father of Elaine (9, 16)

Ban: A king in northern France, father of Lancelot (3, 7)

Beaumains: see Gareth (11)

Bedivere: A Knight of the Round Table, and close friend of Arthur (1, 3, 17, 20)

Bertilak: A knight with magic powers (10)

Black Knight: A knight who fights Sir Gareth (11)

Blanchefleur: A lady loved by Percival, also the Grail Maiden (15, 18)

Blue Knight: A knight who fights Sir Gareth (11)

Bors, King: A king friendly towards Arthur in northern France (3)

Bors, Sir: A Knight of the Round Table, witness to Galahad finding the Holy Grail (17, 18, 19)

Bryssen: Nurse to Elaine, who tricked Lancelot (13)

Carados: Brother of Sir Turquin who was killed by Sir Lancelot (9)

Damas: A wicked knight who holds his brother's lands (8)

Ector: Foster father to Arthur as a boy (1, 2)

Elaine: Daughter of King Bagdemagus, one of Morgan le Fay's ladies (9)

Elaine: Daughter of King Pelles, and mother of Galahad (13, 16)

Gaheris: A Knight of the Round Table, Arthur's nephew, younger brother of Sir Gawain, son of King Lot and Queen Morgause (6, 9, 17, 19)

Galahad: A Knight of the Round Table, The Grail Knight, son of Lancelot and Elaine, grandson of King Pelles (13, 16, 17, 18)

Gareth: A Knight of the Round Table, Arthur's nephew, brother of Gawain, son of King Lot and Queen Morgause (11, 17, 19)

Gawain: A Knight of the Round Table, Arthur's nephew, eldest son of King Lot and Queen Morgause (5, 6, 9, 10, 11, 13, 14, 16, 17, 19, 20)

Gonemans: An old knight, teacher of Percival (15)

Gorlois: Duke of Cornwall and first husband of Igraine (2)

Gorvenal: A wise man and teacher of Tristan (12)

Green Knight: A magic knight, see Bertilak (10)

Griflet: A Knight of the Round Table (4, 17)

Guinevere: Wife and queen to Arthur (5, 6, 9, 12, 13, 14, 16, 17, 19, 20)

Gurman: King of Ireland, father of Iseult the Fair (12)

Hector de Maris: A Knight of the Round Table and half-brother of Lancelot (9, 17)

Igraine: Arthur's mother, wife first of Gorlois and then Uther (2)

Iseult of the White Hands: Wife to Tristan (12)

Iseult the Fair: Daughter of King Gurman of Ireland, wife of King Mark of Cornwall, lover of Tristan (12)

Joseph of Arimathea: A merchant who brought the Holy Grail to Britain (17)

Kay: Foster brother to Arthur and Steward of Arthur's household (1, 2, 9, 10, 11, 15, 16, 19)

Knight in Green: A knight who fights Sir Gareth (11)

Knight in Red-Gold Armour: A knight who is killed by Percival (15)

Knight of Tarn Witherlane: A knight bewitched by Morgan le Fay, brother of Ragnell (14)

Lady of Lyonesse: Wife of Gareth, sister of Linnet (11)

Lady of the Lake: See Nimue

Lancelot: A Knight of the Round Table, father of Galahad (7, 8, 11, 13, 15, 17, 19, 20)

Lodengrance: A king and father of Guinevere (5)

Lionel: A Knight of the Round Table, brother of Bors, and cousin of Lancelot (9, 17, 19)

Linnet: Sister of the Lady of Lyonesse, wife of Gaheris (11)

Lot: King of Orkney and father of Gawain, Gareth, Agravaine and Gaheris, husband of Morgause (3, 5, 6)

Lucan: A Knight of the Round Table, brother of Bedivere (20)

Marhout: Irish nobleman, killed by Tristan (12)

Mark: King of Cornwall, uncle of Tristan (11)

Melias: A knight on the quest of the Holy Grail (17)

Meliot: A Knight of the Round Table (9)

Merlin: A wise man, magician and adviser to Arthur (1, 2, 3, 4, 5, 8, 15, 16, 19)

Miles: A knight killed by Sir Pellinore (4)

Mordred: A Knight of the Round Table, son of Arthur (19, 20)

Morgan le Fay: Sister to Arthur and Morgause (8, 9, 11, 14, 20)

Morgause: Sister to Arthur and Morgan le Fay, wife of King Lot (5)

Nanciens: Hermit, wise man and keeper of the Holy Grail (17, 18)

Nimue: Also known as the Lady of the Lake (4, 6, 7, 9, 20)

Onzlake: A knight whose lands have been taken by his brother (8)

Pelles: King of Carbonek, also known as the Maimed King, father of Elaine and grandfather of Galahad (13, 16, 18)

Pellinore: A Knight of the Round Table (4, 5, 6, 7)

Percival: A Knight of the Round Table (7, 14, 16, 17, 18)

Segramore: A Knight of the Round Table (9)
Ragnell: Wife of Gawain, sister of the Knight of Tarn Witherlane (14)
Red Knight of the Red Lands: A wicked knight (11)
Rience: A king who fights against Arthur (5)
Rivalin: Neighbouring king to Tristan's parents (12)
Rual: Follower of Tristan's mother, who brings up Tristan (12)
Tristan: A Knight of the Round Table, nephew of Mark (12)
Tor: A Knight of the Round Table, son of Sir Pellinore (5, 6)
Turquin: A wicked knight, enemy of all Knights of the Round Table (9)
Urience: King in North Wales and husband of Morgan le Fay (8)
Uther Pendragon: Arthur's father, and high king before Arthur (1, 2, 5)
Uwain: A Knight of the Round Table, son of King Urience and Morgan le
   Fay (8, 9, 17)

AUTHOR'S NOTE

The question most often asked about King Arthur is, "Did he really exist?" The answer has to be that no one really knows. But in all probability there was a high king in Britain who for a time united lesser kings and lords to fight the invaders from other lands after Roman rule was ended. Whether this king was called Arthur or not is open to debate.

If Arthur was a real king, are the stories about him true? They are legends which means they have a foundation of truth. But they have been told and retold over many hundreds of years by travelling storytellers long before they were written down. Each time they are told the storyteller chooses how best to hold the interest of his audience, and so there are endless variations.

Sir Thomas Malory wrote his version of the stories he collected about King Arthur over five hundred years ago, and drew on a great many earlier writings, as well as relying on the oral tradition. I have used his book *Morte D'Arthur* as my main source of reference, but some of the tales in this book are not found there, namely *Sir Gawain and the Green Knight*, *Sir Gawain's Marriage* and part of Sir Percival's adventures. All these can be found in other medieval writings. My version of the story of *Tristan and the Fair Iseult*, is drawn from several sources. The more recent retellings I have particularly enjoyed are *Stories of King Arthur and the Knights of the Round Table*, by Roger Lancelyn Green (Puffin Books 1953), *The Sword and the Circle*, by Rosemary Sutcliff (Bodley Head 1981) and *The Tale of Sir Gawain* by Neil Philip (Lutterworth Press 1987). But there are many more available, not least T. H. White's brilliantly imaginative *The Once and Future King* (Collins 1938).

Why do the stories of King Arthur and his knights have such enduring appeal? They contain all the best ingredients for good stories – magic, action, adventure, clash of characters, jealousy, love . . . . but there is more. They tell of a time when the people were facing dramatic changes. Not only had order been removed from their lives after four hundred years of Roman rule, but the old beliefs of magic, of superstition and ancient religions were being challenged and replaced by new beliefs. Merlin stands for the old wisdoms, and Arthur as a Christian king represents the new thinking of an alternative modern society. But above all it is the people in the Arthurian stories which continue to fascinate succeeding generations. Each of the central characters has a weakness, a flaw, which cannot be concealed even in the glittering and idealistic court of Camelot. So King Arthur's vision and dream of perfection, is destroyed from within.

There are many more stories of King Arthur and his knights which have not been included in this collection. It is my hope that some of you will go on in time to discover these in the rich Arthurian literature that is part of our heritage.

LINDA YEATMAN
Cambridge, September 1990